The
Lemon
Grove

The Lemon Grove

Helen Walsh

Doubleday

NEW YORK   LONDON   TORONTO   SYDNEY   AUCKLAND

Copyright © 2014 by Helen Walsh

All rights reserved. Published in the United States by Doubleday, a division of Random House LLC, a Penguin Random House Company, New York.

www.doubleday.com

DOUBLEDAY and the portrayal of an anchor with a dolphin are registered trademarks of Random House LLC.

Book design by Maria Carella
Title page photograph by Andrew Wakeford/Photodisc/Getty Images
Jacket design by Emily Mahon
Jacket photograph by Mark Borthwick/brigitta-horvat.com

Library of Congress Cataloging-in-Publication Data
Walsh, Helen, 1977–
    The lemon grove / Helen Walsh.—First edition.
        pages cm
    I. Mothers and daughters—Fiction.   2. Majorca (Spain)—Fiction.
3. Domestic fiction.   I. Title.
    PR6123.A464L46 2014
    823'.92—dc23   2013026681

ISBN 978-0-385-53853-4 (hardcover)   ISBN 978-0-385-53854-1 (eBook)

MANUFACTURED IN THE UNITED STATES OF AMERICA

10 9 8 7 6 5 4 3 2 1

First Edition

For my brother, Guy

But suddenly, after these tranquil nights, the weather broke.

—George Sand

The
Lemon
Grove

1.

The sun drops and with it the distant hum of life starts up again. Families and couples weighed down with parasols and brightly patterned bags begin the trudge back up the hill road from the beach. A moped weaves in and out of the slow tide of bodies.

Jenn stays dead still as the weary beach dwellers pass close to the villa. They do not see her sitting on the low stone balustrade of the terrace, hidden among the lengthening shadows of the lemon grove. Their faces are hard to make out but their beach bags and sarongs catch the falling light as they move slowly past the trees. Only one small boy spies her, lagging behind his parents as he drags his inflatable dinghy along the dusty road. Jenn throws him a little-finger wave. The yellow dinghy scratches to a standstill and hangs there by its cord, shifting slightly in the breeze. The child bares a small bar of teeth, then suddenly aware of the distance between himself and his parents, sprints off up the hill.

Jenn puts down her book, tilts her head back, and closes her eyes. From the pine-clad cliffs above, she can hear hikers. They speak in German but from their anxious tone and pitch, she comprehends: Hurry, they are telling one another, we need to get down before the light goes. She knows the cliff walk well—a good two hours from here to Sóller. Two hours of staggering vistas and sheer drops to the rocky coves below. More cars and mopeds pass by. The hikers come into view: a group of stout middle-aged women in robust walking attire. They take the smooth, stone steps down to the road, then stop to pass a water bottle around. They share a joke, but the relief in their voices is evident. Refreshed, and with a new resolve, they strike out for the village. None of them notices her: the woman in the white cotton dress. If they were to glance back they might see Jenn drawing her knees to her chest, locking them with her arms, and looking up as she tries to find the last embers of the sun, to hang on to the moment. She likes the sense of being here, yet being invisible.

✻

She opens her eyes. The first thing she sees is the stone balcony of their bedroom above: the slatted wooden shutters, wide open, the light spilling out of their room emphasizing the sudden shift to evening. The air is beginning to cool. The mosquitoes will be getting in, colonizing the cold white walls, biding their time until later, but she can't be bothered. She doesn't want to move. Up there, Greg will be sleeping, or reading, or showering. For now Jenn is happy here, alone. One more chapter, then she'll go in.

She picks up her book again, *Reprisal*, a Scandi noir thriller. All her young workers at the nursing home have been raving about it but Greg is right: This particular author is no Pelecanos, and for this she's grateful. The last thing she wants while on holiday is to be stretched or challenged. This one is all ravishing blondes in fear of a serial killer. She shuts the book—it is no longer possible to make out the print. She gets up and stretches. Most of the beach traffic has gone now. Through the silence, she can hear the spit and snap of a bonfire. She pictures the hippie kids down on the beach, drying their clothes, cooking their supper. She watched them early this morning, casting out their line from the rocks, time and again reeling in silver, wriggling fish. Boys with straggly beards and bodies scorched from a summer living off the land.

She'd jogged down to the cove at first light. A relic of the moon still hovered above the mountains. The crunch of her feet on the shingle brought two of the beach kids out of their cave. They tried to ward her off with a look, then a joke. And then another boy appeared, naked. He yawned and stretched, lit a cigarette, turning to face her full on. His eyes sought hers, his dick hanging between his legs, mocking and superior, half erect like a threat. She felt a jolt of indignation. If it was solitude they coveted, why pick *this* beach? Resolutely, she peeled off her T-shirt, wriggled out of her shorts, and plunged into the sea. It was cold. A dirty gray mirror under the low morning light. For the first few strokes she could barely breathe. Then, striking out, she was overcome by a sense of liberation as she found her rhythm. She swam out, farther and farther, until the first fingers of sunlight stroked her scalp.

Back on the terrace at Villa Ana, when the sun was high and the beach overcrowded, she saw them once again, making their entrance from the cave-den. Two girls were with them this time. From such a distance, they looked like they'd been sprayed gold. They threw off their sarongs and stretched out their lithe, naked bodies along the flat surface of a rocky overhang, as little bashful as if they were in the privacy of their bedroom. Jenn watched her husband cast a brief side-long glance, so swift that, if you didn't know him, you'd think he hadn't noticed them at all. But Jenn did know him, and his "micro-leching" still made her smile. She'd raised an eyebrow—not to chide him but to empathize. The girls—slim, toned, and young—were exquisite. He looked away: found out, embarrassed.

❧

It's dark now, but still she stays. She can hear the distant bleat of goats drifting down the ravine. Here and there, villas with huge glass façades light up the brow of the hillside. All over the valley, the windows of small stone fincas flicker to life. Hidden amid the olive groves by day, they show them-selves now as their eyes light up, ready to start the night watch over the Tramuntana.

Nothing moves. The darkness deepens. Jenn shivers, intoxicated by the magic of the hour. The road is no longer visible. The first stars stud the sky. A wind rises, and borne on it, familiar sounds of industry from the restaurants in the village above, the clang of cutlery being laid out, ready for another busy evening. She rubs her belly where it is starting to gnaw. It's a good kind of hunger, she thinks, the kind she sel-dom experiences back home; a keen hunger that comes from swimming in the sea and walking under the sun. They've done plenty of that this past week, and they've drunk plenty, too—wine, beer, brandies, liqueurs—they've felt as though they've earned it, Jenn and Greg. And yesterday, after Greg turned in for the night, she sat by the pool and sparked up one of the

Camel Lights she'd found in the kitchen drawer. The kick of it, dirty and bitter, fired her up, made her light-headed.

The temperature drops. The dark hangs damp in her lungs. Sea dampness: salty and lucid and nicked with the scent of pines. Grudgingly, Jenn accepts that time is up. She goes inside to find an inhaler and chivy Greg along. He's out on the balcony, fielding a call on his mobile, a glass of brandy hanging loosely from one hand. He's showered, dressed, scented; his dark, grizzled beard trimmed. He's wearing his cream linen suit—he brings it out with him every year. It's the only time he ever wears it, his gentleman-abroad look. The suit is a little tight around his broad, heavy shoulders these days, but he looks the part—august, though somewhat too formal for arty Deià, she thinks. She hangs by the sliding doors. He's talking to Emma. She feels a tightening in her throat as she listens to him trying to cajole their daughter. She moves out to the balcony and indicates with a two-fingered tap to the wrist that they'll need to leave soon. She reaches over, takes the brandy from his hand, and drains the glass in one emphatic hit. He gives her an admiring glance, smiles.

"Can you ask Emma to pick up some dental floss?" she says. "The silk one. Can't get it over here."

Greg holds up a finger and shakes his head, not so much a rebuttal of her request as a plea for quiet. Emma is taking him to task over something or other and he is doing his usual thing of tiptoeing around her, taking the path of least resistance. Jenn puts down the empty glass, holds her palms to the sky, and rolls her eyes. She steps inside to locate her inhaler. She came away with three—now there are none. She's certain she left one on the floor by her side of the bed. She turns out the solid wood drawers, gets down on her knees to search beneath the bed where, in the absence of rugs, the cool hardness of the ceramic tiles bites right through to her bones. She tips out her makeup bag, noisy in her frustration.

Greg hisses through to her, "Under your pillow!"

Not one but all three of them placed neatly in a row.

"Oh for fuck's sake," she says. She blasts once, twice; better.

He holds up a hand to silence her while increasing the pitch of his voice. "Now Em, worst-case scenario Jenn and I are out . . ."

It kills her, that. All these years on and, when it suits him, whenever he senses a scene, he drops the "Mum."

". . . take a taxi to the village and try Bar Luna. Benni's bound to be there. He has a key."

She makes a big thing of closing the shutters, putting on her jacket. She observes herself in the wardrobe mirror, puts a hand to her mouth and snorts. She bought this white cotton dress in the village store yesterday morning. It was a pure impulse buy, something she wouldn't dream of wearing at home. Yet it's the kind of floaty, classic, *broderie anglaise* frock she'd always imagined herself pottering around Deià in if they moved out here for good. Eyeing herself in the shop's mirror, she liked what she saw. She was elegant yet enigmatic and, yes, sexy; a perception no doubt helped along by the interior candles that shaded her skin a copper brown, the musky incense, the piped flamenco, and the cute gay assistant who came up behind her to lift her hair from her shoulders and whisper, "*Qué bonita* . . . Your eyes are the color of amber." Now she feels duped. She drags the dress back over her head, and her loosely tied-up hair falls to her shoulders. She is gratified to spy the label still intact. She hangs it in the wardrobe and straightens out the creases. She looks at herself again, her deep cleavage accentuated by her tan and the spiced auburn shade of her hair, colored only this morning, and she decides that, fuck it, she's going trashy for one night. Gregory may well tut and bite his lip, but she's on holiday and she's showing off what she's damn well got in tight black jeans and a low-cut silver T-shirt.

As she dresses, she sees that Greg has twisted his upper body around the chair frame to observe her. He makes gestures with his hand that indicate a preference for the dress and her hair worn up. With her jeans pulled halfway up her thighs, she shuffles closer to the wardrobe, takes the dress out for one last appraisal. Even at half price, seventy-five euros was no bargain; and even with the label intact, she anticipates a struggle getting her money back from the campy assistant. She could easily envisage that charm turning to bitchy disdain. She holds it against herself in the mirror. Elegant. Safe. Middle-aged. She'll never wear it again once they're home; she should wear it now, just for him.

He is still watching her. She can hear Emma losing patience with him.

"Oh, poppet, it's fine," he cajoles, and turns his gaze away from his wife. "I'm sure Jenn can live without floss for a week or two."

She places the dress decisively back in the wardrobe and returns to wriggling into the jeans. Was she like that as a teenager? Probably, given half the chance—but she was blighted with acne at Emma's age, she was nowhere near pretty enough to get away with it. She shuts the wardrobe door a bit too loudly and leaves him to it. She clumps downstairs. They'll be late now, whatever.

She takes the last cigarette from the drawers in the kitchen, unhooks the stove lighter from the whitewashed wall, and moves out into the lemon grove. The stark white petals on the overhanging vines glow fluorescent in the dark. Her night vision plays tricks on her: She picks out goats grazing in the grove that, on closer inspection, are no more than tree stumps or bushes. Last night, tipsy from the shots of *liquera manzana* that accompanied their bill, Jenn coaxed Greg into walking home along the river path. But even beneath the brilliance of the moon, they were forced back onto the road, the rough path made all the more hazardous by loose stones and jutting roots. Tonight they'll be taking it easy. No matter how fulsome the welcome or how insistent the offer of nightcaps, on the house, tomorrow they must wake with clear heads. Tomorrow, a different kind of holiday starts.

She squats on the rough, dry grass. Lights up. Sucks the smoke deep into her lungs and holds some back on the exhale, popping out a sequence of smoke rings. How will it be, she wonders, playing gooseberry to a couple of teenagers? And what of this boy, Nathan? Nate. The way Emma says his name irks her—curt, territorial, and loaded with significance, as though *Nate* were a species in himself, one that she herself had discovered.

Jenn has met him, once, a few weeks back, if that awkward exchange could be classed as meeting him. Up until then, Emma had been referencing Nathan with increasing regularity, but thwarting her parents' invitations to tea, dinner, lunch, whatever. It came as some surprise, then, when she got home from a late shift to find Gregory reversing down the drive with a youth she took to be Nate hunched up in the back. He was wearing a beanie hat tugged down over his eyebrows, his jacket zipped up to his chin. It was dark and he kept his eyes glued to the back of the passenger seat, so she barely got a look at his face. She tapped on the window and made a bumbling gesture with her hand to indicate he should come over again—soon. Even from there, she felt Emma's annoyance at her clumsy intervention. The boy flashed a meek smile but Emma stared straight ahead into the darkness, poking at her father to drive on. Later that night, when they got back, Emma said nothing to her—she sat between her dad's legs, the two of them spooning ice cream from a tub, thick as thieves. Jenn had taken herself off to bed, needled at how easily Greg let Emma exclude her these days. Yet it was she whom Emma turned to when she needed an ally over this—the holiday: "You *have* to talk to Dad. He said no, he won't hear of it . . . Nate *has* to come to Deià. All my friends' parents let them take their boyfriends on holiday. Dad's living in the dark ages. You saw him, Mum! Boys like him don't hang around waiting for you. He's *bound* to meet someone while I'm away."

Jenn couldn't help but bridle at "all my friends' parents"; these were families who only technically holidayed together. They took their relatives, friends, colleagues, neighbors, and respective au pairs away with them, Jenn reckoned, because deep down, they couldn't stand one another. But she didn't venture this to Emma. Instead she focused on Nathan. The gauche bush baby she'd glimpsed in the back of the car. He did not look like the type of boy who'd start putting it about the moment his girlfriend's back was turned. "Em, come on. *You're* the one who's going on holiday. It's going to be twice as tough for him. And in spite of what your friends' parents say, I still think it's a little soon for him to be coming away with us. You've only been dating a few months."

Emma was inconsolable. There had been other boys before, but they were nothing compared to this. This was different. This was big—the one against which all future relationships would be measured. Jenn could empathize; she'd been there herself at a similar age. Looking back, she could see that hers had been a manipulative little shit, the lead singer of some dismal shoe-gazing band, and the sex, like the music, was blurred and badly improvised. Yet she remembers each and every beat of it. She would have walked through fire for Dan Matthews.

"Please? Can't you make Dad change his mind?"

"Oh, I don't know Emma... We'll need to meet with Nathan's parents first."

"I'll get his mum to ring you right now!"

"I haven't said yes yet."

"Oh, Mum! You're the best. D'you know that?"

Emma only ever called her that these days when she wanted something. Somehow that hurt more than the slow, inevitable retraction of the word itself.

✖

She regrets it now, crumbling so easily; regrets grinding Greg to submission. The pair of them had worked so hard to be able to afford this particular villa, in spite of Benni, the villa's owner, ramping up the price year after year. He knew what he had, Benni. He knew that they needed it. And with the new dean arriving in September, there was uncertainty over Greg's ongoing role at the university too. Was he still head of English? The former community college had only stepped up to full university status five years ago, but already there was a new board with new, business-driven ideas. There was a pressure on Greg that hadn't been there before; there was more teaching, more admin, PhD students to supervise, and he was now expected to adopt a more hands-on role in upping the annual student intake. So yes, they *needed* their annual fix in Deià, at their beloved Villa Ana. Jenn was determined it was going to be special this year; she imagined they might drive the entire spine of the Tramuntana, from Deià right through to Pollença. Emma was old enough now to enjoy the hippie markets of Estellencs and Fornalutx, maybe the modernist museum in Sóller, too. They could lunch under the grand old orange trees in the square, then she and Emma could browse the boutiques in the old town. She was going to buy Emma something symbolic—a pendant, perhaps, or a bracelet. She wanted something that acknowledged their journey together, their unusual and very special bond. Yet she wanted something peculiar to Majorca, too—a gift that spoke of the memories they'd made on the island.

⚜

So it was settled. She and Greg would fly out a week ahead and Emma would move in with Greg's mum. They could have their boring adult time discovering hidden coves and falling fast asleep after long, lazy lunches—then Emma would come out and they'd spoil her to bits. But it was no longer just

Emma flying out. Now, tomorrow, they would be opening their door, and their holiday, to a stranger—and no matter how much she tries to tell herself she's done a good thing here, Jenn simply cannot shake off her misgivings. She should have stood her ground with Emma. She should have said no.

It is cold now. Up above her, more stars spike the sky. A bat flits past—there, right there, then gone. Observing the house from outside, lit up, its solid shutters absorbing some of the light from the moon, she's stricken with nostalgia for these last few days. Already there's a sense of loss. This week—their week—has shot by. It's as good as over.

✣

They park on the lip of Deià, by the Robert Graves Foundation, then walk the gentle incline to the village. The main drag is buzzing already, people strolling from café to café, perusing the menus or lingering at estate agents' windows to ogle mind-blowing villas with infinity pools, villas they can never own. Candles are being lit on the terraces of tapas bars, and all along the curving road, stout wooden doors in stone walls open up to reveal bijou restaurants with giddying panoramas. From their patio table at Jaume they'll be able to see right down the gorge, past Villa Ana, and out to sea.

They pass the grocery store where they buy bread each morning. The store is closing for the evening and dark-skinned men are ferrying in crates of fat furry peaches from the roadside. Jenn lingers on the pavement, turning out her old leather handbag, filled with junk—brushes, lipsticks with their tops left off, unopened mail—as she tries to find space to squeeze in a couple of peaches for tomorrow's breakfast. Greg hooks his arm around her back and strokes her rib cage with his thumb, ushering her away from the grocer's.

"Quick," he says.

"What?"

Too late. The slovenly, florid-faced man standing in the doorway of Bar Luna has spotted them. He hails them and hastens down the steps, pipe in mouth. Greg strides on but Jenn is trapped.

"Benni. Hi."

His thin, fussy mouth clamps down on his pipe and he nods once, slowly, his eyes raking over her as though he's caught her and Greg in some terrible lie. He looks as though he's been drinking since lunch. A breeze sends a strand of oiled gray hair flickering across his face.

"Again! You eat out *again?*"

He chuckles to let her know he's teasing, but there is a curve of disapproval on his mouth as he puffs his pipe and rocks back and forth on the balls of his feet.

Jenn forces a smile.

"Our last night of freedom, Benni. Emma arrives tomorrow."

Greg is forced to a standstill farther down the road. He tilts his head to the sky, unable or unwilling to disguise his impatience as he waits for her to kill the charade. Benni comes closer, his yellow teeth bared like a donkey's.

"So soon? The party come to an end?" The sour push of his breath blows the strands of hair away from his face. It forces her to take a step back. He wags a finger. "No more misbehave now, eh? Eh!"

He unleashes the full yellow smile and, as he tries to focus on Jenn, reels backward into the road. She seizes her chance and steps past him. Benni shouts after her, down the street.

"But why you eat out when you could be eating al fresco on your terrace?"

She catches up with her husband—who is livid.

"I don't know why you indulge him, Jenn."

Benni stops following them and stands in the middle of the road with his hands held out.

"I tell you! Maria come cook for you. Half the price. Under your own stars." They reach the restaurant. "And you don't have to dress like the Fitzgerald novel." He cackles loudly then coughs.

This last bit is clearly aimed at Greg, and Jenn feels him stiffen. She stifles a smirk and hurries him inside Jaume.

"Fucking clown," Greg mutters, and the family waiting to be seated turn their heads as one. Greg's fury has flushed a scarlet streak right across the bridge of his nose. Jenn giggles as she cranes herself up to kiss it.

"Shall we eat?"

�֍

The restaurant is split into two parts: an airy interior with huge plants and large terra-cotta tiles, and a small outdoor terrace, overhanging the ravine. Miki, the Basque maître d', strides over, arms outstretched. He kisses Jenn on each cheek, standing back to inspect his loyal customers.

"My friends, my friends!" He lowers the flat of his hand toward the floor and pulls a half-sad, half-puzzled face. "But what is this? No little girl?"

Gregory chortles. "Emma? Little? Wait until you see her! Arrive tomorrow—not so little."

They all laugh as Miki shows them through to the terrace, the incident with Benni forgotten now—but Jenn feels little gaiety. Once again, the notion brews that in a few hours this part of the holiday—the them part—is done.

"You tell her, Mikel sends his best."

"Maybe arrive Emma in this restaurant." Greg smiles. "Arrive in Deià with boyfriend."

"The boyfriend? Little Emma? No! *No!*"

"Yes, Miki. Now Emma is big girl."

"So sad. But good time arrive, yes? Next few days the weather is very hot."

Miki gestures toward the sea as he flaps out Jenn's napkin.

"Last year is crazy," Greg says. "Many storm. This? Much better."

The waitress at the next table shoots Greg a baffled look. Jenn laughs. She loves the pan-European pidgin Greg adopts when they're abroad—she loves him all the more because he has no idea that he does it. They've been placed side by side so they can drink in the view together, but there's not much left to swoon about now, save for the hulking black silhouettes of the Tramuntana, crouching squat and immense over the village as though waiting for it to make its move.

Miki sets down two kir royales and a little plate of hors d'oeuvres: a slice of carpaccio speckled with foie gras shavings and a miniature spinach-and-anchovy tart. The pastry is very thin and deep brown, hot to the touch. He gives a loving commentary on each dish as he serves it, and all tension slides from Jenn's shoulders.

"And *this?*" Ceremonially, he places two vials of lurid green broth in front of them. "Beautiful little taste of the garden. Is, how we say . . . *asperge?*"

"Asparagus!" booms Gregory.

"Ah yes. Asparagus. Little soup. Very beautiful . . ."

He kisses the tips of his fingers and Jenn wants to do a little clap for joy. She's overwhelmed by the sense that this is rare; it's unusual; it's what holidays are *for*. She feels like hugging Miki, and he seems to comprehend. He draws a deep breath and makes intense eye contact as he reels off tonight's specials. Jenn is salivating over a braised asparagus served with pear, or simple, grilled *gambas y ali oli* starter when Miki crouches down and whispers in her ear.

"Now, Jennifer. Please. The rabbit leevers. I must recommend to you this fantastic taste to start with. I know you will love."

He jumps back to his feet, this time hovering over Greg.

"And for both of you magnificent persons, for the main course, I have to persuade you of the fantastic mountain kid. Fresh, like this, slowly roasted with the fragrant rosemary"— Miki pronounces the *a* hard, *fragg-rant*—"and served with a little taste of the sea, our special salty, green sea vegetables." He takes one pace back, as though introducing a chamber orchestra. "Perfect."

She feels like applauding his performance. Both of them had planned on eating fish tonight—week two was going to be the healthy week—but this is a restaurant that understands the imperative of fat; fat is where all the flavor is. Greg lets his menu drop to the table. He holds his hands out wide.

"Sold, *señor*. Rabbit livers and mountain kid it is." And before Jenn can give it one last run-through in her mind, he's added: "Times two."

Greg beams at her. She registers the flicker of hesitation on Miki's face, so she winks to let him know: It's fine. Just for tonight, it's okay.

They let Miki choose a local Rioja and, true to his word, it's rich and spicy and, with the first sip Jenn is able to kick back and banish all niggles and woes, and all thoughts of tomorrow. The night and the billions of stars that now spatter the sky still belong to the two of them. To her. To hell with taking it easy, she thinks as she takes a gutsy slug. Tomorrow's tomorrow.

It's almost two by the time they get back to the villa. Neither of them is ready for bed. Greg brings blankets and candles out to the pool, and two cold bottles of San Miguel. Jenn sits by the edge, rippling the moon with her big toe. Greg sits behind her, his knees pulled up at her ribs, his arms draped loosely around her waist. They hear laughter from down on the beach and Jenn remembers the naked hippie girls, slim and flawless and fully aware of all eyes upon them. She half turns and snuggles her cheek into Greg's chest and reminds him.

"Which one did you fancy?"

"Both."

She slaps his wrist. "Who was it who said, youth is wasted on the young?"

"George Bernard Shaw."

"No—it was definitely Robbie Williams."

Greg laughs and kisses her neck. His hand slides under her top. The suggestion of sex hangs there for a moment but she is heavy from food and drink and she delicately removes his hand. He seems content enough; he strokes her hair, scratches her scalp. They sip at their beers and look at the stars and she kisses him firmly on the mouth; a kiss that says "time for bed."

✠

She is asleep. An insect is buzzing at the periphery of her consciousness. Does Greg get up? Was that a book that just slapped the wall? The gnat is no longer buzzing. The next thought she has is that, somehow, it's morning. Greg's side of the bed is empty. Strong sunlight is poking through the shutters.

They are on their way.

2.

"Did you not hear us coming?"

Jenn is lying by the pool, her book rent at the spine and splayed across her face, its pages fused to her skin. The voice—its hurt and angry timbre—sits her up. How long had she been asleep? She hadn't meant to doze off. This was just a quick top-up to bronze her strap lines while the sun was still bearable. And even then, as she opened the book across her face and shut her eyes, she told herself she was only drifting for a bit—cogitating, coasting the outer veils of consciousness, but definitely not asleep. She'd been aware of the scrape of the broken gate in the gravel, Berta the maid shouting *Hola* from the steps. She'd extended an arm and twiddled her middle fingers back in greeting—she'd get up and fix them both a glass of lemonade in a minute. But then, for a while, she'd given herself over to the buzz of cars snaking down to the beach, imagining what lay in store for each. But this last car, theirs, turning into the long dirt track and crunching its way toward Villa Ana? She'd been dead to it.

She props herself up on her elbows and blinks back the fierce light. It takes a moment for her eyes to acclimatize.

Slowly the silhouette standing before her takes form. Emma looks different somehow; it's only a week since she waved them off from the back of Greg's mum's car, but she's altered. She's swapped her usual jeans and T-shirt for a short but elegant bandeau dress that she's teamed up with sandals and a sixties-style sun hat. The outfit is brand-new and cost way more than the fifty pounds Jenn gave Emma, so she wouldn't have to borrow from her nana. But the transition is not just sartorial, is it? Her face, the way she's carrying herself. Has she lost weight? Are those highlights in her hair? Jenn tries not to stare at her.

"Did you not hear us coming?"

What is this? She knows that tone, knows it too well. She's being berated—but what for? Jenn suddenly twigs and sits up straight.

"Did you not have money for the taxi? Shit . . . Your dad has the euros. Is he still not back from the supermarket?"

A trickle of sweat wriggles down her nose as she leans over and gropes for her bag. Her naked breasts hang loose. She snatches up her vest from beside the sun lounger. Her skin is hot and sticky and, as she tries to force her arms through, the cotton twists and tightens, snaring her upper body in the diving position. With her breasts now trapped under the hem, farcically round and exaggerated, she struggles to untangle the fabric. She concedes defeat, pulls the vest back over her head and starts again. Emma eyes Jenn's freckled shoulders; runs her eye over her body.

"Taxi? What taxi? Dad came for us."

Jenn is shot through with anger but strangles it there and then. She takes her time, slowly feeds her arms through, one at a time, then inches the fabric down with her thumbs. The ritual gives her time to compose herself.

"That must have been a nice surprise."

"Surprise? Hardly. It was all arranged last night."

This time Jenn can't suppress the pang of hurt. "All arranged?" *When* was it arranged? While she was in the loo at the restaurant? It was certainly never discussed. She swallows it, straightens her back, gets up, and envelops Emma in a hug.

"Well, anyway—you're here! You look fantastic." Emma pulls away, still eyeing her askance. Jenn takes no notice, claps her hands together. "So, honey. Where are you hiding him? Where's your man?"

"Inside. Unpacking."

Her tone is glacial.

"Oh. Okay. So. Lunch? How about a Spanish omelet?"

"Tortilla. It's called tortilla." She seems to enjoy enunciating precisely: *torrh-tee-ya.*

Again, Jenn squashes the impulse to rise to the barb, counters it instead with an extra shot of jollity.

"I can chop up some tomatoes and those jalapeños you love, instead of the onions, if you want?"

Emma tunes out, turns around to face the villa where Gregory is wheeling a suitcase across the terrace. Without turning back around she murmurs, "Thanks. But we ate on the plane."

Did they have an argument? Is that it? Is this how it's going to be for the rest of the week?

"Come on. I'll help you unpack."

Emma removes her sunglasses; little, sullen dents appear in her chin. She looks close to tears.

"Emma?"

"Don't act like you don't know!"

"What? Did you and Dad have a quibble, honey?"

"You *knew* we were on our way! You had *loads* of time to . . .
to *prepare* yourself! Do you *know* how that made me look?"

And now she understands. "Honey—I'm sorry. Really. I
fell asleep."

Emma turns her head around and holds the position.
Eventually she brings it back, she lowers her chin, her top lip
trembling.

"Lying there . . . like that. It's not what you should be
doing at your age. Do you know what you look like?"

No, but she can guess. Emma thinks she looks unseemly,
ropy, cheap. Emma is very near quivering with pique. Jenn can
feel it coming. She focuses on her book on the ground, calmly
picks it up, turns it over as though considering it for the first
time. But when it comes it is worse, it is much worse than any
of those jibes.

"You look common. Really, really common."

Unable to staunch the tears, Emma flounces off down
the path.

Jenn does not attempt to call her back. She needs a glass
of wine. She picks up her towel, wraps it around her waist,
and, barefoot, hot-treads the flagstones back to the villa.

❧

She doesn't want to go inside. She stops at the standpipe,
runs the tap, and realizes in a flash that it's this she's been
dreading. Not the arrival of the boy, nor yet the relinquishing
of her me time with Greg. For the past week she's been living in ever-tightening anticipation of the continual treading
on eggshells, the constant adjusting to the weather vane of
Emma's moods. It's been like this for the last two years, since

she turned thirteen, but Jenn hoped that falling in love, properly, for the first time, might give Emma a different perspective, encourage her to think beyond the confines of her own selfish needs. Maybe Greg is right, maybe she should cut her some slack. Maybe she has cut her too much, tried too hard. Jenn laughs bitterly and scoops a handful of water to her dry lips. She snaps off the tap. She can admit it to herself now— she's scared, scared of the tension Emma's mere presence can bring, even to a place as idyllic as this.

She steps away from the standpipe and becomes aware of a figure in one of the upstairs windows, looking down at her. She puts her hand to her eyebrows to block the hard light shafting down, but there's no one there.

❧

Greg is in the kitchen, tearing hunks from a baguette. Jenn can tell from the slight resistance of the flesh that the dough is fresh, still warm. She pulls a piece off for herself, chews it slowly, the aroma and the soft, moist feel of it making her reach for seconds immediately.

She clears her throat. "Emma's mad at me."

"Oh really? How come?" he says.

He smiles with half of his mouth.

"Don't!" she snaps. She is in no mood for levity. "You could have warned me."

"How? By beeping the horn?"

He leans forward and kisses her on top of her head. She shirks away.

"Why didn't you tell me you were going for them?"

He turns away, sheepish. "Last-minute decision. Anyway"—he winks, turning back to her—"the beach is awash with topless women. Your peep show will make for a handy prelude for them both."

"*He* didn't see me though, right?"

"Don't think so. I was too busy dragging *his* bloody suitcase out of the boot to take too much notice, though." He pulls her toward him, cups her chin gently. "Don't take it to heart. You know how it is at that age. Em's just keen to make the right impression." He drops his voice, moves his mouth in close to her ear. "A bit bloody intense, anyway."

"Who? Him?"

She jerks her head at the ceiling above them. Greg steps back and nods. The few times Greg had given Nathan a lift, he'd come away relieved, if a little frustrated. Taciturn, is how he'd described him, and she knew what Greg meant by that. The boy was your typical surly teenager. So the mixed message was that while Nathan might lack the magnetism to seduce his daughter or lead her astray, he would neither enrich nor inspire her teenage life. Jenn had the impression that Greg was happy enough with that; did she now detect some kind of a sea change?

"Did you get my text?" he says.

"Oh, hang on—the one telling me you were on your way?"

"No. The one about the unmentionables."

She'd laugh, usually, but something about the way he says it makes her shudder. Jenn takes a glass from the cupboard, opens the fridge.

"So, go on—what's off the menu?"

There is no wine. She sighs, hoofs the door shut with her bare foot. Moves to the sink, fills the glass with water, drains it in two gulps but remains at the sink. She stares at her reflection in the window. Greg comes up behind her. It's his coaxing voice, trying to make light of a tricky situation.

"Okay, let's see. There's to be no talk of gymkhana, ponies, lacrosse, or any other activity you'd associate with a girls' school."

A *private* girls' school, Jenn wants to correct him. Fees circa eight grand per annum, fees she resents paying when there are so many perfectly great comprehensives on the doorstep, fees she's long since given up bickering about. She forces a smile and turns to Greg. She has no wish to bicker today.

Greg draws himself up. "And under no circumstances do we *ever* refer to her Chemical Romantics phase."

Jenn softens and tweaks his beard. "Chemical *Romance*," she corrects. "Anyway, I thought that was how they met—at a gig."

"Not a Chemical Romantics one, it would seem."

Jenn laughs, pleased that Gregory is on her side for once. Whatever the crime and however hard his daughter nails herself to it, Emma can always depend on Daddy to dredge up some excuse for her: *She's working too hard. It's her monthly curse. Her mother died giving birth. Her stepmother is always at work. She has abandonment issues.* Jenn has long since learned to accept it for what it is; the legacy of grief is a chronic affliction, not curable but manageable. And Jenn has managed it well. She wipes a cluster of crumbs from the corner of his mouth. "Where is he anyway?"

Almost on cue, the wormed wooden beams of the kitchen ceiling give out a little creak and, moments later, there's footfall on the stairs. There's laughter as the lounge doors creak open, feet slapping across the terrace, and the riotous splash of bodies as they hit the pool.

"You sure? Doesn't sound too intense to me."

She pours herself another glass of water. He takes it out of her hand, glugs deeply then passes it back.

"Yeah, intense. Intense in the way that young people can be. The inherent corruption of the establishment. Minimum wage. Workers' rights."

"He's fifteen! What does he know about workers' rights?"

"Seventeen, it would seem." Greg raises an eyebrow. "Quite adamant that he's not going to university."

Jenn snorts, shakes her head, undoes her towel from around her waist. Gregory lowers his face to her and mimics: "The notion that university encourages critical and independent thinking is a myth. Academic institutions only stifle our naturally autodidactic nature." He pulls a face and points at her, thumping the table so hard that the glasses jump. "Such institutions show us not *how* to think but *what* to think!"

She stifles a guffaw; spits her water back into the glass. "He actually said that?"

"No. She did."

They raise eyebrows at each other. She tears another hunk of bread for herself.

"I'm off to shower, anyway. Hopefully the sun will have thawed her black mood by the time I come down."

She pads off upstairs, wondering if her husband would have thought her intense when she was seventeen.

3.

She is in the kitchen when she first sets eyes on him. Since Emma's strop, the teenagers have made themselves scarce, glimpsed only in snatches and via intermittent bursts of sound: the creak of the wheelbarrow as he pushes her around the rutted gardens; the plunge of bodies into the pool; wet feet on the veranda; and those longer stretches of silence, filled in by the puttering of iPods, the beeping of phones. They are invisible and yet their presence is everywhere: They possess the entire villa. Jenn can hear them shuffling around upstairs. She calls from the bottom of the stairs: "I've made fresh lemonade. Lovely! Want me to bring some up?"

There is a fluttering in her throat as she anticipates the scurry of feet, the frenzied stretching and bending of limbs as clothes are pulled on in haste, but the voice that comes back is bright and innocent.

"Thanks. We'll be down in a mo."

So Emma is no longer mad at her, but they do not come down.

Jenn prepares lunch. She slices what's left of the bread, the crust already hardened by the heat, and she dices and blanches potato cubes, chops and fries up tomatoes, peppers, jalapeños. There's half a tin of sweet corn in the fridge that she's tempted to tip in, but instinctively, she knows that "tinned" will grate with her daughter. She digs out a big ceramic bowl, remembers where she's put the eggs she bought from Berta. "No refrigeration," the maid had warned, ticking her off with her forefinger. Jenn had left the fresh-laid eggs in the cool of the walk-in pantry, just in case one of them hatched. She breaks the eggs into the bowl and begins beating them. She can hear Benni talking loudly to the gardener—when did *he* sneak in? Doubtless news of Emma's arrival has filtered through, and he's come to take his fill. From the kitchen window she can see a slice of Gregory's head under the umbrella, the bald oval on his crown reddening under the midday sun. His head is erect and motionless behind his newspaper. She feels his irritation at Benni's invasion, even from here. He's trying to pretend Benni's not there, but she knows Greg won't be taking in a word of the news. She carries on beating the yolks.

"Hi."

The voice, coming from directly behind her, takes her by surprise and the bowl slips from her grip. She services the silhouette in the archway with a brief nod before turning to the bowl at her feet, spinning but miraculously unbroken. It doesn't bear thinking what monetary value it might suddenly accrue if Benni had to replace it. Some of the yolk has splashed onto the waxed stone floor. She squats, simultaneously dabs at it with a tea towel and tries to assess if there's still enough in the bowl to make an omelet—there is—before her gaze moves back to the archway. The silhouette lingers a moment before stepping fully into the kitchen. Jenn is conscious of herself not quite controlling her reaction. She can feel her face slacken. She tries to compensate, looking down at the bowl and keeping her hands clamped tightly to her hips, as she gets to her feet. Surely this cannot be the same kid—the sulky bush baby from the back of the car? He takes a couple of steps toward her, then stops dead. He is wearing a pair of plain blue swimming shorts; otherwise, he is naked before her. He is muscular but graceful with it, balletic. He is shockingly pretty. She is aware of the seeming impropriety of registering these details—he is seventeen—and yet she cannot tear her eyes away. He seems either faintly amused or embarrassed. He drops his head.

"I didn't mean to startle you. Sorry."

His accent is hard, at odds with his feline, feminine face. His voice jolts her out of her holiday idyll and for one moment she's back at work, she's back on the streets of Rochdale, where she grew up.

"Can I help you with that?" he says and glances from the tea towel in her hand, down to the kitchen floor, where a line of ants is already marching toward the yellow slick. Jenn stands there, frozen in the frame as the boy steps toward her and passes around behind her, to lift the smoking pan from the stove.

"Oh shit. *Shit!*"

He is smiling now. The air is thick with charred fumes; the smarting in her eyes and lungs propels her, finally, into action. She takes the pan from him, sets it down by the sink, and throws open the window. Benni is standing outside, grinning—a basket of oranges and lemons in his hand. He waves cheerily; she doesn't reciprocate. When she turns back, the boy is down on his knees, mopping up the mess with a wet tea towel. She observes the tendons in his arms stretching as he wipes, back and forth. His shoulders are sprayed with freckles; his hair, thick and dark, cropped at the sides and weighty on top, the haircut all the young boys have—except this is no boy is it? He may be only seventeen—but he's a man.

She reaches down and takes the towel from his hand. Her voice catches in her throat.

"Leave it—it's fine!" It comes out as an imperative—not her intention—and she compensates with a smile. "Really, Nathan. You go and find Em. I can take care of this."

She drops the towel in the sink, wipes her hands on her shorts. The boy gets to his feet. He's going nowhere. Now what? Should she embrace him as she might any other guest, kissing him chastely on either cheek? He preempts her dilemma by holding out a hand. She shakes; his fingers are youthful and slender, the skin accustomed to holding hands with teenage girls.

"So. How was the flight over?"

Though she tries to control her voice, she can hear the accent of nervousness in it. She moves away from him and puts on a pair of rubber gloves, if only to *do* something.

"There were babies," he says. "And a hen party."

Paah-eh. The accent jars with her again. She'd had no hint of this from the couple of times she'd chatted on the phone with Nathan's mother, in the run up to him coming away. She was softly spoken rather than well-spoken and there was no trace of a Manchester accent. She wonders what Emma makes of it. Is this why she kept him secret for so long? What do her school friends make of him? What about Harriet Lyons and the old gymkhana set? They'd be jealous for sure. They'd taunt her no end over Nathan's accent, if only to reassure themselves that even if he was theirs for the taking, they would not want him. And she knows Gregory. He may talk the talk of a left-leaning libertine, but he's a snob. No wonder he's been so reticent about Nathan.

She looks up, expecting a grin. His expression is serious; his green eyes wide and his pupils huge, like he's been running. He perches himself on the edge of the big pine table; he looks strangely at home. He reaches around to scratch his neck. Jenn's eyes are drawn to the thatch of dark hair in his pits.

"Any of that lemonade? Sounded good."

Her ears are hot as she moves to the fridge and fetches the cold glass jug. She finds a glass, pours his lemonade. His eyes never leave her. He drains it in two gulps, his throat expanding like a snake's as he swallows, mechanically.

"So ... what do you think of Deià?" she says, dropping her eyes to the floor. Even before he answers, she's cursing herself. How many times had she joked and bitched with Emma about parents who find conversation so unnatural that they have to kick-start it with a "So ..."

He smiles, as though he understands.

"Well—there's a lot of money," he says. But before she can counter, he hits her with those huge, earnest eyes. "Love to come here in the winter though, me. Bet it's wild."

Jenn licks away a drip of sweat from her lip and eyes him.

"It *is*! We came here once in December when Emma was only little. It's a different island—every bit as beautiful, but frightening, you know?"

He is grinning—is he mocking her? She's trying too hard. She reins in her enthusiasm, strives to keep her voice on an even keel.

"It's, I don't know, you're so much more aware that it's an *island*."

He's nodding now. Closes his eyes in agreement.

"I came here in June once," he says. "Rained the whole time."

"Here? To Deià?" She can hear the surprise—the near disbelief—in her voice. She goes to redress it, but he interjects.

"Here? Ha! My ma would love that, yeah!" He reveals a row of very white, surprisingly small teeth. "Nah, other side of the island. C'an Picafort, we stayed."

"I don't know it. Sounds nice."

But Jenn does know it and she feels her neck burning up. She ignores the urge to touch it.

"No," he says. "It's a dump."

She looks away, over-scrutinizes the bowl as she picks it up and turns it around and checks for chips or cracks. A strange, unsettling energy crackles through her, just like that empowering rush she'd felt on the beach with the hippie kids the other morning. Yet this low strumming unsettles her. It zaps the skin on her neck, like the static of their old TV. She is relieved—grateful even—to hear the slap of Emma's flip-flops across the tiles. She breezes into the kitchen, devastating in an electric-blue bikini—another new addition to her holiday wardrobe. A gold chain belts her slim waist; a dazzling fake sapphire studs her navel. Yet again, Jenn finds herself irked by the question of who's paying for all this—she can hazard a good guess, and it's not Emma's beau. But overriding these petty concerns is a sense of awe at her daughter's womanly figure. Where did those legs come from? And the breasts.

Emma plants a kiss on Nathan's lips and crosses one ankle over the other as she tugs at his wrist.

"Come on. Beach. Last one in the sea buys lunch."

Nathan's earnest gaze stays on Jenn, seeking not just her consent but her approval too. Whatever burned in his eyes before—whatever she imagined was there—has withered.

"Think Jenn's making lunch," he says.

Emma whispers in his ear, loud enough for Jenn to hear. "We've only just got here. We can eat with the oldies tonight."

Jenn tries not to show that she's stung.

"Go on—you two make a run for it before Dad kidnaps you."

Without a hint of protest they're out of the door, Emma's bikini briefs barely covering her bum. Jenn sighs and gives the heavy cast-iron frying pan a shake. She sniffs at the charred vegetables and scrapes the lot into the bin. She loiters at the window and watches them pad down the path. As they disappear from view, Nathan's arm drops from Emma's waist to cup her small buttocks.

4.

They find the lovers seated at the far end of the beach restaurant on the rocky precipice. They're side by side, looking out to sea with their feet up on the low, whitewashed wall. That was me once, thinks Jenn, that was us. Wistful, she reaches down to find Greg's hand and squeezes. Nathan's arm is draped over the back of Emma's chair, his thumb tracing an intimate curve from her neck to her shoulder. She wonders what Greg makes of the tender vignette as they come up the stone steps and into the restaurant. Does the same thought crash through his mind? Are they? And if so, for how long? Because the last time she looked, the last time she thought to look, Emma was still a kid. The highlights, the waist chain, the navel stud—these are all red herrings, surely. This is a girl with a row of teddy bears at the end of her bed. A girl with a full thatch of pubic hair.

They skirt the line of diners waiting to be seated and, ignoring the stares, pick their way across the floor. A large matron, sweat popping from her brown forehead, comes flaring toward them, wagging her finger. Gregory doesn't break his stride but Jenn drops back to explain. She points out the teenagers and the waitress softens at once. She smiles and guides Jenn to the table, reeling off some platitude about *amor* and *jovenas*.

The table is fashioned from a hunk of driftwood and set on two stone pillars. Gregory wedges himself in at the far end of a wooden bench, his back to the sea. Jenn hovers, waiting for Emma to make room, but she's in a world of her own. She clocks Nathan's hand drop from Emma's neck. He slugs his beer from the bottle and, once Gregory is settled, slides his hand over to her bare thigh where it rests, a finger's width from her crotch. Jenn feels a clenching of the stomach, a quickening of the pulse. If they're not doing *it* then they are doing everything but. She strides to a nearby table and brings back a white plastic chair. Seated, but still irritable, she puts on her reading glasses, picks up a menu.

"You guys ordered yet?"

The teenagers shake their heads. She has to lean back to avoid the sear of the sun. As Nathan scans the menu, she sneaks another look: his broad, slender frame; the pale green eyes spaced too widely apart, perched on the side of his face like a horse's; the big wide mouth and his little white teeth, whenever he smiles. And his hair—masses of it. A beautiful boy, she concludes. Emma was right not to leave him behind. As though reading her mind, Emma links arms with Nathan and rests her head on his shoulder.

"Shall we just get a cheese sandwich? Maybe some fries to share?"

Greg gives a snort. "Really? What happened to *gambas a la planchas*?" He turns to Nathan. "She won't thank me for telling you this but it's all she's talked about for months. She dreams about the seafood in this place, don't you Em?"

Emma shoots him a withering look. Nathan turns to Emma, pecks her on the cheek.

"You go ahead, honest. Order what you want." He lifts his head, a little too slowly and self-consciously, Jenn thinks, and smiles apologetically. "I'm vegetarian."

"Oh, I see," Greg says. "No worries."

"I'm not," he smiles. "Worried, I mean . . ."

She feels a brief, protective frisson shoot through her—it's not often she sees Greg floundering like that.

"The stuffed peppers are good," she says without looking up.

Greg tries to catch the plump señora's eye. Jenn runs her finger down the menu.

"The salads are okay here, too. They pad it out with the grated onion though," she smiles. "Never a good sign." She pauses to let each of them in on the joke. Greg has his arm in the air now, as though he's hailing a taxi. Jenn plows on, compelled to keep talking. "Oh! Tell you what, though—they have a wood-burning oven, don't they Greg? I had an artichoke-heart pizza the day we came out. One minute you're in Manchester, the next you're sitting here, eating the most amazing food."

Nathan's smiling at her. A young waiter arrives at the table, scowling. Greg leans back, stretches his arms behind his head, and claps his hands.

"Yes. Know what I fancy? A nice crisp bottle of rosé. Any takers? Goes with everything, rosé!"

"Can I get another beer please?" Nathan says. His "can I get" grates on Jenn and tells her that these two are mere babies. She and Greg should head off. They're cramping their style.

"Actually that's a great idea," Greg smiles. She knows he doesn't mean it. "*Quatro cervezas, por favor!*"

Emma smiles her thanks. Her father has only this year started to allow her a small glass of wine with her evening meal, so she appreciates the efforts he's making not to show her up. A dog circles the table hopefully; lies down on the floor to lick its balls. On autopilot, Jenn turns out her bag for an inhaler. She locates it, puts it to her mouth, and squirts, all in one go.

"Don't suppose you brought any spare?" Nathan says.

"No. Sorry. Do you need one?"

"I should be okay."

"We could get you an appointment at the village doctor? Couldn't we, Greg?"

She can feel Greg tensing, see the thought bubble forming as his lips purse and his mouth disappears in his beard for one moment: Who will pay? Does Nathan have insurance?

"It's not that serious," Nathan says. "Not really. Not even sure if it *is* asthma. Had a bad bout of bronchitis last year; lungs have never been the same since."

Emma straightens up, ready to seize her chance.

"Global warming is what's done that. Seriously."

"I don't know, Em," Jenn says.

Greg booms across them. "Nonsense! What does global warming have to do with asthma?"

Nathan speaks quietly but with calm authority. "Well, obviously no one knows for sure, but anyone can see the changes in the weather patterns over the last few years. Like all the rapeseed we've been seeing. That mad cycle of torrential rain, sunshine, wind, and rain. It's got to be a factor in the amount of pollens right? And it's not just seasonal anymore is it?"

"I read a very interesting piece in the *New Statesman* suggesting it's more to do with our total reliance on motor vehicles."

Emma has already forgotten her dad's indulgence of her drinking. She's bristling at him now—her eyes glinting.

"What is?"

"The proliferation of new asthma sufferers."

She shakes her head and hisses. "Well they *would* say that."

All eyes are upon her at once; Nathan shoots her a nervous, sidelong glance, but Gregory is enjoying himself.

"Who would, darling? Who'd say that?"

"The Bullingdon Club elitists of the London media."

Nathan seems to be squirming in his seat. Are these his opinions? Emma is growing up, yes, but these are improbable words for her daughter. The dog gets up, pads around to Nathan, who reaches down behind Emma's back to pat it and scratch its head.

"Do you really think that?" Gregory says. "*Really?*" The question is aimed at his daughter, but his eyes are trained on her young suitor. "Aren't you getting your media mafias a bit mixed up? I thought the Bullingdon Club was a Tory haunt, the stomping ground of the old boys' network?"

Nathan looks out to sea, distancing himself—clearly he had not anticipated his sounding board to become a conduit for his polemic.

Emma looks at her father: precarious, defiant. "Whatever … Look. *Observer, Guardian, New Statesman,* all those papers you swear by, right? The supposed voices of the left? None of their reportage is unvarnished fact, is it? It's just *their* interpretation of events, preaching to the converted. Our media establishment is basically made up of Oxbridge white boys from wealthy families."

"I really don't think that's the case these days, darling. If I'm not mistaken the editor of *The Observer* hails from—"

"*That's* not the point though is it?" She talks over him again. Greg remains patient but he's no longer amused. The glimmer in his eye has gone. "Look, if you want the truth, if you want the facts before they're fed through the propaganda mangle, there are plenty of unbiased sources out there these days."

Jenn is still blindsided by *reportage.* She's pleased that Emma is putting her father through his paces and yet she bridles at an image of her daughter nodding in docile agreement with every thought Nathan spouts at her. Still she can't help but be impressed by the boy's broadside. Gregory cocks his head, the game smile replaced by mild exasperation.

"Emma, this isn't the Cold War, you know."

Once again, he shoots Nathan a look. Jenn leans across the table, stretching her arm out to Greg to let him know she's not taking sides against him.

"Emma does have a point though; things have changed massively since you were a student, Greg. Look at the Arab Spring. We watched history as it happened, live, and we witnessed it through the films and blogs of those who were living it. The newspapers basically just editorialized what we already knew."

Nathan nods in agreement and smiles when she catches his eye; she feels a pulse of excitement beating beneath her skin. Gregory draws himself up.

"So in that respect, at least, Gil Scott-Heron was wrong. The revolution was, after all, televised."

He seems pleased with himself, she thinks—as though he's won some mammoth debate. The beers arrive, and Jenn seizes the opportunity to steer the group back into safer seas.

"You know, I was thinking we might head up to Sóller tomorrow. There's a train—"

Emma cuts right across her. "You know Nathan is a blogger," she blurts out as though she's been restraining herself all this time. "All the local bands want him on their guest list."

Nathan seems to flinch at the telltale "local." Gregory sits back and takes a sip of his beer, eyeing Nathan with a sneer.

"How does that work, then, Nate? How does one blog about a local gig? Or do you just present the unvarnished facts: band arrived, band played, band left." He chortles at his own witticism.

Nathan smiles back. "I think you might be getting confused with all this modern stuff. I'm allowed more than 140 characters."

Emma smiles and hugs him, then without any announcement or apology, jumps up and takes herself off. Jenn watches her all the way to the queue for the restaurant's sole toilet. Maybe she is on her period, after all.

A basket of bread arrives, along with fat green olives, balsamic, and oil. At the same time Greg's phone starts to vibrate. It dances along the table. Greg holds it up, looks vexed, puts it down. He twirls it around on the tabletop, then sighs and slips it in his shirt pocket. It's the fourth time this afternoon his phone has rang; the fourth time he's ignored it. He can sense her looking at him, and he makes a face as though to say "What? We're on holiday!" He leans across and grabs a crust of bread, tears off a shred, and dips it in oil. He nods, makes loud appreciative noises, the discussion—and the phone call—forgotten for now. Nathan, for his part, seems happy enough for peace to descend. He eyes the bread hungrily but restrains himself until Jenn offers him the basket. Greg is craning around and behind, trying to get the waiter's attention again. He gets up and smiles down on them, as though to acknowledge and atone for his testiness.

"I need wine!" he smiles. "Flint-dry white wine—and lots of it."

He strides off to the bar. Alone with Nathan, Jenn feels the weight of the silence. She goes to initiate conversation but pulls up short, imagining how she'll sound. Nervous. Unnatural. Eager to impress. If this were twenty years ago and they were in the bar of her local, rolling cigarettes and sinking pints, waiting for the next band to take the stage, there'd be no such lull in conversation. She'd be inclined to disagree with everything he said, but she'd wish that she'd said it first. Somehow it's strange seeing Emma so completely in thrall to this kid. The way she hangs on his every word—his world, really—it's not healthy. It's not her. Jenn should tell her; she wouldn't listen to her though.

Nathan drums his fingers on the table.

"Was that really Gil Scott-Heron who said that?"

She wants to grab the opportunity by the throat; chant out the rap at him, word for word. But again, her better self overrules her.

"I think so." She shrugs. "Bit before my time."

Another drawn-out silence. Breathe. Sit back, sip your beer, she tells herself. But her ego is chipping away at her. Tell him! Tell him about the time you hitched down to Bristol to see Nirvana play; only a handful of people had heard of them back then.

"So. You're a blogger? That must be cool."

Cool. How very uncool she must sound. He sits forward. "Probably be passé this time next year. Still."

His eyes are looking directly into hers. She can't hold the look; takes a slug of San Miguel to deflect attention.

"I may be interviewing Nigel Godrich."

"Wow!"

"Radiohead's producer."

"I know who Nigel Godrich is."

"Waiting for it to be confirmed. But I may have to go back home a few days early if it comes off. He's only going to be in Manchester for the day. Well—Media City."

Jenn processes her disappointment quickly, steadies herself, sweeps her eyes across the crowded beach below.

"Emma said that Gregory writes."

His eyes are narrowed like he's testing her. "Yes," is the honest answer, but it comes with a sense of regret. She wonders how much Emma has told him about Greg's novel. Did she mention the string of rejections? Perhaps she should warn him not to bring it up.

"Romantic poets—is that it?"

Jenn smiles her relief, he means the academic tomes, and she relaxes just a little. She is always cautious talking about Greg's work. For one thing, she doesn't know enough about it to proffer an opinion. She wonders if other lecturers' wives are like that—she has never known any to ask. But somehow she feels at ease with Nathan. She settles deep in the chair, reaches for her beer.

"Third generation mainly. Beddoes, George Darley. The ones only academics are interested in. Are you a fan—of the Romantics?"

"Don't mind the band."

He squints, shields his eyes with his hand like a salute. Jenn laughs, leans forward to tap the table playfully. " 'Talking in Your Sleep'? You weren't even born then."

"*Glee* has a lot to answer for."

"Yes. The ironic appreciation of shit."

He smiles at their in-joke but turns away, looks out to the cliffs. She loses him for a moment, then he comes back and eyes her very directly.

"Are you into your music, then?"

Yes, she wants to say. Try me.

She fiddles with the frame of her sunglasses then puts them back in their case and takes another slug of her beer.

" 'Course—but Emma is the real music nut." She smiles and draws the subject to a close by pointing down to the cove. "Tomorrow we'll take the cliff walk and find a cove of our own."

A gang of kids with dirty blond hair charges in and out of the surf, the only movement on the docile beach. Everyone else is sleeping or reading, or suffering the sun. Nathan shifts in his seat to watch them and, as he turns, his leg touches hers. It's no more than a graze, like the scratch of unruly grass along a narrow path, but she feels it like a sting. She pulls her leg away, then overcompensates, swatting at an imaginary fly, and drains the last of her beer, concentrating on a high-gliding gull. When she is finally able to look again, Nathan is still staring out to sea. He hasn't noticed a thing.

The waiter sets down a carafe of white wine, the big glass jug misty-cold and dripping in condensation. Gregory and Emma are on their way back, smiling about something, arms around each other. As the waiter wipes down the carafe, his gaze trails off across the cove. He shakes his head, mutters

"*Locos*," encouraging them to follow his gaze. Two of the hippie kids—a girl and the boy who bared his penis—are scaling the promontory, naked. The girl seems to know all the grooves in the rock formation; she runs up the cliff face like a spider, never once looking up or down. She reaches the top long before the boy. Jenn puts on her sunglasses and observes. The girl's hair is plaited with brightly colored beads. She has full, firm breasts but the rest of her body is as hard as a boy's. She is perfect—and Nathan is transfixed. She's perched on a ledge, high above the sea. Diners, picnickers, passersby are craning to watch her and, cognizant of her audience, she stretches to tie back her plaits, the motion lifting her breasts, exposing their shape and heft. Jenn grabs for her bottle, realizes it's empty. Reaches across for the wine, hoping he will realize, apologize, pour. But he is mesmerized by the girl. The ledge is narrow, barely room to turn, and below is just jagged rock and sea—yet she fixes her hair and turns, nonchalant, as though she's about to step off a slowing bus. She pauses for a second, picks her spot, crouches, shoots out her arms, and dives. There is a collective gasp from the restaurant as she plummets through the air and rips pertly into the sea with a minimal plop. As she bobs back to the surface, there's relieved applause from her onlookers. She makes no acknowledgment, cuts back to the shore with efficient strokes, and hauls herself onto the rock just in time to see her boyfriend make an altogether noisier plunge. He, too, emerges effortlessly, but swims out and away from the beach with powerful ease.

"Who are those kids?" Nathan stares until the girl disappears back into their cave, an awe in his voice that Jenn wants to stub out.

"Euro trash, them. BMW heirs—or IKEA. Can't you tell?

White dreads hanging out at Deià? Don't think so. Trustafarians, slumming it, that lot. Their yacht'll be anchored around the other side of the cliff."

He nods; looks ill at ease as he glances back toward the cave. Emma and Greg arrive at the table. Emma's all smiles now.

"Who's for a swim after lunch?"

Jenn trains her mouth into a smile and pours out two large glasses of wine.

5.

They pick a spot at the farthest end of the rocky cove. A few huge boulders, stacked back against the cliff face, offer some relief from the sun. The sky is clear. There is still no breeze. Out of some girlhood habit, Jenn sits down on the shingle and wriggles out of her jeans, but for now leaves her cotton shirt on. Greg rolls his towel into a pillow of sorts, flexes his shoulders, shifts positions until he can get comfortable on his pebble berth. He closes his eyes, squeezes Jenn's hand, and lets out a slow sigh of satisfaction.

Jenn sits with her back to the rock, scanning the cove for Emma and Nathan, sweeping left to right and back again. Big women with layers of loose, brown skin hanging from their arms swing children through the shallows; they seem totally at ease with their ravaged bodies. A couple of middle-aged guys in microscopic trunks squat among them and one of the women lies down on the shingle right in front of them and self-consciously removes her bikini top. She throws her head back, pushing out her breasts, which are slack and massive. Jenn snorts, twists her head to say something to Greg, sees his eyes are shut, and leaves him to it.

She spots Emma out beyond the families, gently ladling seawater over her knees and shins. Her hair is salt-tangled and corn-yellow in the sun's dazzle. Even with her pale pink skin, she could be a supermodel winding down from a swimwear shoot. Her bikini sequins catch the sun, spraying glitter sparks out across the water. Jenn hides behind her sunglasses, holding up her thriller, its spine completely ruptured now, without taking in a word. The sun glare off the page is too dazzling. Her head is too hot.

He is right across the bay, in the place where the hippie chick dived in. He appears to be heading for the rocks, below the hippie cave, where kids with nets and buckets now patrol the rock pools. He moves through the water in slow, strong strokes. Jenn takes off her sunglasses, wipes them on her shirt, and puts them back on. He pulls himself up onto a little plateau with an effortless grace. He has his back to her. He smoothes his wet hair back. Seawater trickles down his neck and shoulders. He stands and plunges noisily back into the water, cutting through the waves with a mechanical ease. There's no performance—he's exhilarated out there. She follows his rhythmic strokes across the bay, back to the flat diving rocks. He drags himself out again and shambles across the rocks. Jenn's eyes go with him—only to find herself staring at Emma sitting in the shallows. She is being watched, watching him. Sheepish, found out, Jenn waves over, an embarrassed splaying of the fingers. Emma grins and cups her hands around her mouth.

"Come on in!" she shouts. She beckons her over with a scoop of her arm. Gregory, drowsy from the wine, smiles and pokes her.

"Go *on*."

Emma swings the arm again. "Come on! It's lovely!"

Another dilatory prod.

"You should be flattered. I don't hear them calling for me."

Jenn twists her upper body around, pokes him back.

"They know their level."

"Touché. Young Rimbaud's certainly not shy, is he?"

She watches as Nathan guides Emma over the sharpest rocks. They overbalance and tumble into the sea, Nathan laughing, Emma shrieking. She turns back to Gregory.

"They make quite a handsome couple, don't you think?"

Gregory props himself up on his elbows for a moment, observes his daughter and her beau. He wrinkles his nose.

"No. I do not."

"Know what, Greg Harding? You're a snob."

He manages a sleepy sigh and lowers his back down to his pebble pit. She pecks him on his crown.

"But if it's any consolation at all, I don't see those two lasting. Really. So in the meantime, try and cut them a bit of slack. It will have blown itself out by the end of the summer. Let's just hope they last the holiday, hey?"

He rolls over, takes hold of her wrist, and squeezes. "I love you," he says.

She begins unbuttoning her blouse. He reaches for her. She pulls away, smiling, continuing with her buttons. Greg's denim shirt begins to vibrate as his phone rings in his pocket. His face drains in an instant.

"Shouldn't you get it?"

"No. It's just work. Fuck them."

She stretches her arms behind her neck. "Everything okay?"

"After a fashion. They want to know if we can Skype."

"Skype! Why? You're on holiday."

Greg shrugs. "Your guess is as good as mine." He digs out his phone; stares at it. "I should just call them."

She takes it out of his hand; puts it in her bag. "Don't you dare! You're right. Fuck them. You left your phone in the villa and we're lost at sea for the next six days." She throws her blouse over his face. He lifts it off with one lazy finger, eyes his wife in her swimsuit.

"You have the most magnificent breasts. Come here."

She curtsies and picks her way down to the shore.

The water is colder than she'd anticipated. She wades one, two, three steps into the sea then, feeling the shock of the first wave against her groin, flings herself in and stays under as long as her lungs will hold out. When she comes up for air she finds herself in the shadow of the overhang. The dark water is perfectly still and foreboding. She strikes out, keen to get back into turquoise seas, under the sun. She makes slow progress toward Emma in her trademark self-conscious breast-stroke, her head and shoulders erect above the surface of the water. Emma's face splits into a smile as Jenn finally splashes up beside her.

"Isn't this heavenly!"

"Gorgeous."

"Come on. Wait until you see this."

She lowers her head to the water and kicks off, and Jenn follows. Together they swim to a cluster of rocks jutting out of the shallow sea. A shoal of fish darts in and around their feet. Emma treads water, breathless, grinning.

"Told you."

"Beautiful." Jenn smiles back, but she can hear the asthmatic rasp in her voice. Her rib cage heaves under the swimsuit as she fights for breath. She allows the ebb and flow of the sea to drift her backward onto a partially submerged rock ledge and sits back to rest, to regulate her breathing. Emma treads water in front of her, smiling right into her face. She's seldom seen her looking so elated and, somehow, the notion pains Jenn.

"Don't you wish we could stay out here forever?" Emma ducks down like a seal, bobs up on the other side of her. "You should retire here."

"Retire? I'm really that old, you think?"

"I didn't mean it like that."

"What does your man think anyway? He liking it here?"

Emma gives a coy squint. "Said he'd happily live in a cave. We could live off the land."

"He said that?"

Emma nods, warily. Her eyes flash, just for a second. Her little nose is beginning to peel already and her face is sprinkled with sun freckles. You're beautiful, thinks Jenn. I wonder if you know it yet? Emma squeezes Jenn's fingers. So rare is her touch these days that it tips her stomach.

"Thanks, you know, for making this happen."

Jenn is almost relieved when the fingers release her.

"He seems like a really nice boy."

Nathan has moved into their view, back on the diving plateau on the other side of the cove. He's looking in their direction, as though sensing he's being talked about. Emma squints up at her through one eye.

"He is, you know, Mum. He's lovely."

Jenn is conscious of her nostrils flaring, her eyes smarting. She tamps a rising frisson back down and focuses solely on Emma. Her daughter is there, in this moment, within reach once again. Jenn wants to hold her close and tell her: Come back to me. Come back, honey. She smiles and strokes her wet hair, breathing easier again. Greg comes into view behind Emma's bobbing head. He's sitting up, dabbing his brow with Jenn's blouse. She knows him too well. He's hot and grouchy—but too indolent to join them in the sea. Emma follows her gaze.

"Do you think Dad likes him?"

Jenn leans toward her and pushes a loose strand of hair behind her ear. "You know what, chicken? I think he does."

Emma flinches from the hair-tucking and furrows her brow, as though Jenn has overstepped the line again—that vague and ever-shifting line that declares then rescinds their friendship. Emma seems to realize what she's done. Her head is bowed, her face contrite. She lowers her voice and whispers.

"I didn't mean to, like, snap at you before." She gives a little glance up. "After you made it all happen for us. Dad would never have let Nate come away if it wasn't for you. I know that."

Her forearms take her weight on the rock ledge now, her legs gently treading water. Her face is open, ready to give and receive—yet Jenn fears making the same mistake twice. She maintains the distance but bestows a forgiving smile.

"Shouldn't I be apologizing to you, anyway? I'm sorry about that, if I embarrassed you. I really wouldn't have . . . I didn't think you'd be there so soon."

"I wasn't. Embarrassed." Emma eyes her, unsure for a moment. "But I think Nathan was."

"Nathan?"

Emma glances back to where her father lies comatose on the beach. The sparkle has vanished from her face altogether now. "Think I'm going to head back for a nap. Nate and I thought we'd walk up to the village tonight."

6.

Jenn still can't bring herself to go back. She swims onward and out, turning the revelation over in her head. So Nathan saw her topless. How long had he stood there? Why had no one said anything? The more she dwells on it, the more obvious it becomes. Nathan has only ever seen pictures of Villa Ana. The first thing he'd want to do, a boy of his age, is check out the pool. She picks up speed, if only to put distance between herself and the thought of him, but it slides back through her with the spray. She pictures his shoulders, the tight yoke of muscle. Child's skin stretched over his man's frame. She pictures his hands, the veins on his wrists; the feather of hair that trails from his navel to the trim waistline of his shorts. She swims on, curving her path back toward Platja de Deià to avoid the flotsam drifting in on the tide. She can see the hippie girl shinning that shank of rock again. The sun glazes her. She looks like a goddess—mythic and burnished. Jenn turns onto her back to watch her, tarantula-like, scuttling up the cliff face. Gentle waves lap Jenn's earlobes, warming her shoulders, her armpits, as she lies back and looks up at the azure sky and lets the lilting tide carry her away.

The water gets choppy, colder. She flips herself over and is shocked at how far she's drifted from the shore. She slides into a measured breaststroke, eyes on the distant pinprick of the beach café, the green flag billowing easily by the rocks—but her lungs have tuned in to her unease, out there. Her windpipe is starting to tighten, her wheezing becoming more pronounced as she plows on. She thinks the people in the beach restaurant can probably see her, an illusion tossed among the waves. They throng the small terrace, their heads like little bobbing beads on a necklace, but she's too far out to shout. She hasn't the breath to shout anyway, and her arms are too leaden to wave. She rolls herself onto her back again and slowly advances back to shore—listens to the squiggling sound waves of underwater thermals in her eardrums.

The water is warm again. She dips her toes down; the water is still too deep to stand. Back there on the beach lies her tatty leather bag; in it, her lifeline—her iron lung. One blast and she'll be fine. She pushes on. Rocks are visible deep below her, seaweed and anemones writhing in the crags. She lets a foot dangle, and this time she finds a wobbling rocky dais. She lets the water take her weight as she tries to balance on the loose stone slab, crouches low at first, then as the next wave propels her forward, she gets herself up and onto the next big stone. There's a slight drop, but then it's shingle. She's made it; she's back. She wades slowly through the water. She's coming in at the farthest end of the cove, but she's still waist-deep and doesn't have the energy to steer herself left. She lets the tide take her down the path of least resistance. She can barely lift her legs now, when two firm hands take hold of her hips from behind.

"Jenn! You okay?"

Fleetingly, the tide swell drives his groin into her buttocks. She nods but her face must tell a different story. She turns to face him. He's standing there, knee-deep, his eyes all over her. He smiles meekly and offers a hand.

"You sure?"

"I'm fine. Asthma attack," she manages. "Soon as I get my inhaler."

He nods and bends to the task, moving in front of her and draping his arms out behind himself to pull her along. The water drags like tar. She focuses on the sea salt drying to a crust on his biceps. She can no longer feel the shell grit underfoot. Only the fingers squeezing around hers and the thumb kicking out to move across her wrist every so often, keeps her anchored to the ground.

7.

The sky is still low and the tips of the mountains shrouded in cloud as the car strains up the hill. Deià is deserted at this hour. As they pass through the village, Jenn nods at Jaume's shuttered frontage.

"We should book for our last night. The four of us."

"Mmm."

Greg won't meet her gaze and he preempts any further discussion of the subject by staring pointedly out his side window, over-concentrating on the view down to the sea. He'd mooted the idea to Miki in the restaurant the other night, but he's since changed his mind about sharing Jaume with Nathan, and he's cross with Jenn for not running it by him before blurting it out. She stews on it, rankled by him— and yet she empathizes, too. He's touchy about their special place. They have history with Jaume and Jaume with them. She can see how the intrusion of a stranger might spoil that symbolism for Greg.

The road broadens into wide-open countryside, and she gives up musing and abandons herself to the sun-starched fields strewn with golden cylinders of newly baled hay. The lid of cloud has lifted now and the sun is warming the dirty-gray Mediterranean to a shimmering cerulean. Greg veers into the oncoming lane as he cranes his neck around to ogle the villas wedged into the hillside; one in particular has fascinated them for as long as they've been coming here. A car beeps at him, and Greg holds up his hand—guilty—and swerves back to his own side. Emma is more reserved in front of Nathan, but Jenn can still sense her wonderment at the storied casa, standing sentinel over the land. In years gone by she and Emma would make up stories about the exotic lives played out behind those elegant, pine-green shutters. For one moment all four pairs of eyes fix on the traditional limestone house spread over four or five floors, almost as big as a hotel. They once harbored dreams of buying a house on the hill. Nothing as spectacular as the casa grande—but something. Over time, there was a gradual narrowing of aspiration and, for a while, that realization embittered Jenn. Not just the rude unmasking of the vanity of her dreams—*their* dreams—but also because Greg had allowed her to believe that anything was possible. She knows better now. She knows there'll be no fantasy home in Majorca. She knows there'll be no baby of their own. She knows all this yet there is still a part of her not willing yet, not ready to accept it.

They pass the roadside restaurant that they say, every year, they must visit. They reach the T junction by the garage and turn left onto the bumpy old Valldemossa road. Pines spring up and directly outward from the road, splitting the surface and gnarling it with blisters. Greg swerves to avoid the tree roots, holding his glasses to his nose as he negotiates each bump and pothole. Jenn has a flashback to him swinging the wheel from left to right all the way down this road once, sending Emma into fits of giggles. They were a family then. She was Emma's Mummy.

He slows as they approach the market on the left where crones in identical pinafores are already thronging the stalls for bargains. He zaps down the windows, for Nathan's benefit, she assumes, and it is a sight to behold. The accent of the market is on Majorcan heritage crafts and, as they crawl bumper-to-bumper through the little town, each stall lays out artisan wares. There's a pottery stand selling hand-painted sangria jugs; there are wooden toys, porcelain crockery, baskets full of colorful sweets and lollipops; there are fine, made-to-measure shoes, glass-blown figurines, and row after row of local pastries and delicacies. One stall sells only the emblematic *ensaïmada* pastry, next to it a specialist *sobrassada* outlet. The melody of aromas wafts through the window, mingling with the nutty scent of fig leaves that spices the breeze. In her side mirror Jenn can see Nathan's face, dancing. He nudges Emma.

"Doesn't half make you hungry."

"You're *always* hungry."

Jenn makes a thing of being lost to the world outside her window but she steals a glimpse, every now and then. As the road curves up and out of town there's a secondary market in a car park, more colorful and hippyish in feel. It's more for the tourists, this one, with the cross-legged bongo players beating out their Balearic rhythm as visitors browse racks of tie-dye T-shirts, lizard sculptures fashioned from driftwood, jewelry stores specializing in amber and beaten silver. Toward the top end of the car park, there's a whole section of the market displaying the paintings of local artists, and here something catches Nathan's eye. Jenn watches him in the mirror as he cranes his head out of the window until they've almost passed through the town.

They park up on the outskirts, get out, and stretch. Nathan's crimson polo shirt is already sticking to the mounds of muscle beneath his shoulder blades. They walk back down toward the monastery. Greg points over, for Nathan's benefit. "Built as a royal residence, originally," he announces. "Then the Carthusian order took it on as a monastery. That's where Chopin and George spent the winter, year or two before he died."

Jenn and Emma quicken their step—they've heard all this before. Nathan is not so fast. Greg blocks him off.

"George Sand. Have you read her?"

"Never heard of her."

"Oh, Nathan, Nathan, you're missing out. One of *the* great temptresses of the nineteenth century."

Emma stops and turns. "So, not one of *the* great feminist thinkers of the nineteenth century?"

"Definitely not." Greg smiles. "Much more effective man-eater. And womanizer. Chopin died of a broken heart when she left him for that actress."

"Thought you said he died of TB?"

Jenn can sense her husband floundering, and this time she's willing it to happen as she inwardly cheers Emma on.

"Well, cystic fibrosis, technically, but—"

"Ha!"

Victorious, Emma flounces off again. Jenn catches Emma's eye and winks. She can sense her husband blushing behind his beard, muttering some excuse to Nathan. She flits her head around, ready to intervene, but Nathan isn't even listening. He's craning his neck back in the direction they've come from, fobbing Greg off with an "mm" and a "right" as the lecture restarts. Before she can look away, Nathan turns back to her—catches her watching him. She gives him a smile, playful but nervously hopeful of reciprocation. He holds her gaze, but his face gives nothing away. And then he nods and smiles at Greg and skips past to catch up with Emma. He slides an arm around her, steers her away to the other side of the cobbled street. It's not a rebuttal to Jenn—of course it's no such thing. Yet it's confirmation that whatever took place yesterday, took place in her head. He carried her ashore, and that was that. They'd dug out her inhaler, got her breathing back to normal. But once she was fine, she had not been able to look Nathan in the eye. When she did so, it was a hangdog, sideways glance, like a pup expecting to be told no. Then almost immediately after that, Nathan and Emma had made their excuses and headed back to the villa. She and Greg had stayed as the beach began to empty, enjoying the last of the sunshine—that balmy sensation of having nowhere they needed to be. The sting had gone from the day and it was all diffused mellow light and soft slow motion. Greg, soporific, had reached across and she'd taken his hand. Yet all she could think of was Nathan's big hands belting her waist. Nathan, back at the villa, naked. With Emma.

❧

She watches him and Emma conspiring; they'll be off to do their own thing. She tries to close herself to the notion brewing within, and yet she cannot stop thinking about the way he rescued her yesterday. Why does she imagine that, too briefly to register, he'd pressed his pelvis against her? Why can she not drive that notion from her mind? It is madness. It did not happen—not intentionally. Perhaps his dick grazed her bottom, but it was the tide that pushed him; it's impossible to balance on those slippery stones. Why was he hard, then? No. It did not happen. And yet the fact that no one registered her struggle, that she'd managed to swim out so far unnoticed, and that no one thought to look for her—that *did* happen.

Jenn watches Emma lean her head against his arm as they walk, and notes that he flinches a moment before pecking her on the head. Emma faces him for a kiss. The way she looks up at him, God . . .

They share a joke about something. He has her head in a lock for a second, then he shoves her away and slaps her bottom. Emma flips her head over her shoulder, laughing, as though the butt of their joke lies somewhere back here. They gradually increase their pace until it's fait accompli that the four have become two. Greg is more cross than deflated.

"What happened to the plan? We all agreed, didn't we? Market, monastery, lunch?"

"We're not cool enough." Jenn smiles. She says it in jest, but she's bruised by the reality all the same.

She lingers on it for a while, tuning out Greg's commentary as they amble down the town's narrow streets, past blond stone houses toward the shadows of the monastery. She can hear the market, a low hum of chatter like an intermission between acts of a play. The air is cooler here; Jenn's disquiet calms. The cobblestones are waxy underfoot, centuries of footfall polishing them to a dangerous sheen. Greg extends an arm for her to hold on to. He casts her a look that is pure affection, his face creasing into a crinkly smile.

"Never tire of this place, you know? Never."

She shoots back the appropriate degree of empathy. "Me too."

Greg is drawing himself up to make some grand philosophical pronouncement when he's interrupted by his phone. It has rung off by the time he's able to prize it out from his breast pocket.

"Work again?"

He nods; stares at the screen.

"Phone them back."

"I thought you said . . ."

The voice-mail clarion blares out. He clicks his jaw from side to side, still staring at the screen. Jenn hooks an arm around his waist.

"Look. Go and sit on that bench. Call work. Whatever it is, sort it out—then have a little wander. Bit of Greg time." She goes on tiptoe and kisses his nose. "I'll meet you back here in an hour."

She turns and heads down a short flight of steps and goes into a trot, lest he call her back. In the distance, she can still pick out Nathan's T-shirt.

The hippie market is busy with tourists, young folk mainly and a few wizened old men wearing sarongs and sandals. She feels out of place for a minute as she pauses at a stall whose sole output is wood-carved wind chimes. The young assistant with dreadlocks tells her they're carved from the wood of ancient olive trees from the garden of Jaime I of Aragon. He says it with conviction, but it's tinged with embarrassment, as though he understands how ridiculous he sounds, but how often it works. She nods her head slowly, looking about to see where they went. They're over by the jewelry stands, heading toward a stall specializing in tie dyed T-shirts, but there is something about the set of Emma's shoulders that tells Jenn all is not okay. She offers the assistant ten euros for the wind chimes and when he laughs in her face she doesn't hang around to barter; she positions herself at the next stall along, this one specializing in hand-woven rugs. She tucks herself behind a stripy kilim and observes.

Nathan is holding up a T-shirt. Even from here she can tell that it's made from the cheapest fabric possible, yet he's handling it as though it were an object of beauty, holding it in front of him and nodding his appreciation. Emma stands a little way back from him, her arms wrapped around her rib cage, her face tilted to the ground. There is something unnatural about Nathan's posture, it's a little too masculine and contrived—and Emma seems threatened by it.

The *vendedora* leans across the rows of ruched and marbled fabrics at the front of the stall and offers Nathan a different patterned shirt. Jenn can make out no more than her slender, brown arms and the beaded ends of her hair as they swing forward, yet there is something queasily familiar about her; something in Nathan's smile and the self-conscious ruffling of his hair that is priming her for the possibility of trouble.

This particular design is a garish kaleidoscope, but Nathan takes time to consider it carefully before declining with a tactful shake of the head. Jenn slips in and out of the rugs until she's close enough to get a proper look at the girl. It takes a moment for the penny to drop, and when it does she is blindsided with a furious envy. It's her, the hippie girl from the cave yesterday. She is flirting with Nathan and he is flirting right back. And in an instant her jealousy turns to anger, directed not at Nathan, nor the hippie girl, but at herself. It's obscene, it's *ridiculous*, that she's standing here in the first place, spying on them. And yet now that she is, she cannot tear her eyes away. She watches Emma fixing her hair and letting it down as she tries to effect nonchalance. She wants to go to her. And yet, coiling around her protective instinct, slowly strangling all parental concern, is a smug and sinister satisfaction at the sordid role-play.

The transaction seems to be drawing to a conclusion, the hippie girl is bagging up the T-shirt, and Nathan is shaking his hand to indicate that she should keep the change. Jenn feels her bowels loosen a little, her throat start to prickle. She moves in the opposite direction, back toward the road, past the wind-chime guy who on seeing her repositions himself at the side of the stall and holds out the chimes, already bagged up. She pushes past him and crosses the road back onto the cobblestones and hard right into the alleyway. She can see Greg, right at the top, walking in slow deliberate circles, still on the phone. He looks stooped, smaller somehow.

8.

The teenagers are late. Jenn has offered to wait up in case they need a lift back from the village. She's promised Greg that no more than one small glass of Rioja will pass her lips, but one glass has led to another and she's flopped out on the dusty sofa. The crime thriller, beach-wrecked, has been slotted away in Benni's library. She will never finish it. On her lap, in its place, is *Walden*, a book she adored in her youth; a book of which she's been a passionate advocate in debates with Greg. She is revising her opinion now, as she drifts off.

She sits up: something innate and chemical tripping her from sleep. Dry-mouthed and feeling the first seeds of a hangover she hasn't really earned, Jenn gets up and goes to the sliding doors. A pair of headlights are moving closer to the villa, and now she can hear the diesel thrum of an engine. Out there, the darkness is as dense as a coma. There is no moon. Way beyond the ravine, the clap of a hunting gun reverberates through the mountains. It was sounding off early this morning, but the shots seem more pronounced now in the darkness. As the ricochet echoes to nothing, she abandons Thoreau and takes herself upstairs before they stumble in.

She is brushing her teeth when she hears the slam of the taxi doors, the scrape of the gate below. There is a sniffling from outside. Is that Emma crying down there? Jenn steps up onto the bathtub and peers down through the window's grille. It takes a moment for her eyes to adjust: one, two silhouettes. Not human, though—a couple of donkeys have strayed into their garden and are standing beneath a tree with their heads lowered to the ground, possibly asleep. Way up the hills, as though flying through the rolling slabs of black, the receding taxi's brake lights blink red at each twist of the switchback. She hears it again—not tears but laughter. Emma is giggling and the knowledge of it plants something raw in her stomach. Jenn snaps on the air conditioner and climbs into bed. Gregory stirs. His breath boozy, stale, he asks, "They back, darling?"

She squeezes his hand. He's out again within seconds. Jenn lies there, unable to shut down, listening to the wind rise, the crash of the waves, the hiss as the water sucks back through the shingle on the shore. The sound and fury of the tide takes her back there once again. Thoughts of the cove; thoughts of him. She bumped into him in the corridor before, on his way out. Handsome in his jeans and white vest. Brown arms. From Nathan, there wasn't even a flicker. He'd smiled as he passed her, and a pain like a hunger pang shot through her.

It's a while before they come inside the house. What have they been doing out there? They do not bolt the kitchen door. She hears the skid of the refrigerator door. A stool knocked over, more giggling, then footfall on the stairs. They seem to hover outside his room for a while. Jenn torments herself with the image of his hands on *her* tiny waist. No soft padding on Emma's hips; skin as smooth as a newly hatched egg as his fingers prize their way under the hem of her denim shorts.

But then Emma is passing—no, she is *stomping* past— their room. Is she imagining this? No. Her bedroom door slams and she hears muffled sobs, as though Emma is buried beneath her sheets. Should she go to her? No. Jenn closes her eyes and tries to shut it out—all of it. She craves the sobering reality of a new day. But she's thirsty now; her brain is fully engaged and she can't shut down. She fumbles out for the glass on her bedside table, tilts it, but it yields only a dribble. She lies there, staring out into the dark, but she knows she won't sleep until she's cleared her throat.

She gets out of bed, irritated by her husband's snoring. The bedroom floor is cold, the air cool. She switches off the air con and goes downstairs. As she steps into the kitchen she sees that the big oak outer door has been left wide open. She curses the pair of them as she heaves it shut, slotting the large iron crossbar in its groove and planning the conversation she will have with Greg tomorrow. Will he rebuke his daughter as he would her? Of course not.

As she comes back into the kitchen she smells the drift of tobacco smoke before she sees him. He's there with his back to her, sitting on the steps to the terrace, staring out at the night sky. She's unsure whether to say something or inch back upstairs unannounced.

"Hello Jenn," he says. He doesn't move. A jet of smoke wafts upward.

She freezes, says nothing. He stays dead still for a moment longer, then flicks the cigarette out onto the terrace and twists his upper body around. He smiles, gets to his feet. His eyes are black sockets in the darkness but she can feel his gaze all over her. He stumbles slightly as he pads toward her. She can smell beer on his breath. She knows she must speak up soon lest her silence be misconstrued. She struggles to inject authority into her voice.

"Make sure you lock the door."

He is less than two feet away. She takes control, turns, and walks to the foot of the stairs. He hesitates, then kicks his shoes across the kitchen floor. Sure now that he has her attention, he heads down the steps. The terrace light trips on, isolating him in a bright white halo. She should go upstairs, back to bed, to where her husband sleeps in deep oblivion. But no—she goes back to the kitchen to slam the terrace door shut, to let their houseguest know he's overstepping the mark. As she grabs the handle, he turns to face her. He tugs off his T-shirt, peels down his jeans, drops his boxers. She does not look away. Naked, he crosses the terrace to the pool's edge, his muscular bottom backlit in the neon blue of the underwater lights. He hesitates on the lip of the pool and turns, just long enough for her to see his dick, before gliding cleanly into the water.

Jenn takes the stairs two at a time, closes the bedroom door, leans against it, panting hard. It's nothing her inhaler can temper this time. She climbs into bed, stricken by the proximity, the very presence of her unwitting husband, queerly reassured by the barrier he forms. Greg's long arm loops around her and pulls her close. She lies very still, her thighs squeezed tight, ankles locked together. She tries to snuff it out. No use. Her stomach flips her over and inside out, the pulse between her legs fervent, painful.

She drags and guides his hand, moves it down and under the rim of her shorts. His fingers hang there, somnolent, too blunt to submit to her will. She ducks beneath the covers to rouse him. Hears the kitchen door slam shut as she takes him in her mouth.

9.

The shutters are closed, but as soon as she wakes, Jenn senses a full-bellied sky out there—she can feel it in her chest, too. The peal of goat bells on the hillside confirms what she already suspects: There's a storm brewing.

Jenn drops an arm down the side of the bed, fumbles for her morning inhalers—two blasts of pink, then one of the blue.

She pads out onto the balcony. The tiles underfoot are cooler than usual. The gray weight of the sky seems to hover just above the sea, and way up beyond the village, a veil of black shrouds the mountain. From inside the bedroom she hears movement: the rustle of sheets, a hard stream of piss hitting the toilet basin. Her stomach tightens. Seconds later, he stumbles out to join her.

"Morning!" Greg trills. He is grinning at her. He ducks down and kisses her deep on the mouth. Jenn stops short of flinching away from the stark unfamiliarity of her own embarrassment. "Sleep well?"

There is devilment in his eyes and something else, too. Awe? Whatever—last night's bombshell has blown his mind.

Greg is gay and light of step and she cannot stand it. Fearing a reference to the blow job, or worse, expectation of a repeat performance, Jenn extricates herself from his grip and leans over the balustrade. She looks out to the horizon.

"Not really, actually. My chest was awful. Must be a storm due."

"It'll be the pollen, darling." He advances on her again, kisses the back of her neck. "It's going to be dry but overcast this morning; blazing hot sunshine by this afternoon." He slides a hand under her top, squeezes her breast too hard. She squeals and jerks away—if Greg takes umbrage, it doesn't show. He slaps her bottom playfully. "Perfect weather for the walk. We should do it today."

She nods. "Sure."

Her attention has been snagged by movement on the terrace below. Greg follows her gaze.

"Morning!" he shouts down.

The boy looks up to them—at her—nods, then heads on to the pool. He is carrying her novel.

Jenn drives up to the village for supplies. Emma has not emerged from her room—still sleeping, or sulking, she supposes. Nathan is lapping the pool. As she reverses out of the path and turns into the dirt track, she spies him in her rearview mirror levering himself out of the pool on the flats of his hands. He stands, poised, watching the car. She rounds the first bend—out of sight, out of mind. The boy is Emma's problem, not hers.

The village shop is opening as Jenn pulls up on the single yellow line outside. The papers and fruit have not yet been laid out. She decides that today they can do without both. She shuts down the engine and goes into the shop. A boy no older than Nathan stops her on the threshold, a palm held up like he's stopping traffic.

"*Diez minutos*," he says, rather brusquely.

"Oh, right," she says, more inconvenienced than annoyed. Can she be bothered going back to the village car park? It wasn't just finding the coins for twenty minutes' parking, it was the whole rigmarole involved in turning the car back around. She might as well just carry on toward Valldemossa and use the mini-market instead. She pictures Greg's face as he unpacks the bags and finds prepackaged croissants rather than the oven-fresh bread and pastries he's been coveting. She strikes a deal with him in her head: She'll grab a coffee in the bar across the road while she waits for the shop to open, but if the parking wardens arrive on their mopeds, she's off. Greg will have to make do with a microwave breakfast.

The café's terrace, perched above the main road, is still grubby from a busy Saturday night: plastic chairs blown over, tables sticky with spilled drinks, the ground strewn with cigarette butts, and the smell of stale fried garlic wafting out from the dark cavern of a bar. Jenn takes a seat as far away from the door as possible but close enough to the steps to make a hasty getaway should the traffic wardens arrive.

The crone who serves her is laughably surly, viewing the early-morning trade more as a nuisance than a fillip. There's no "*Buenos días*," or "*Hola, señora*," just a curt "*Sí?*" But for Jenn the experience is mitigated by the orange juice she's served, so fresh and thick it feels as though it's being pumped straight from the citrus grove behind. The coffee is also good; potent enough to zap away the dregs of her hangover—full of bite but by no means bitter. Why can she never get coffee like this in England? Even the pioneering little independents in West

Didsbury don't come close to this. She sits back, sips slowly at the orange juice, luxuriating in the tang of each slurp. Such simple pleasures, she muses—so profound in their impact. The sun pokes through the cloud cover and Jenn tilts her face toward it. She stretches her arms out, elbows down, and holds her fingers in a loose yoga pose. She imagines a different life, of mornings that begin with a swim in the sea, a coffee on the terrace instead of traffic jams and orange juice from a carton. It's a nice fantasy while it lasts; the sun ducks back behind the clouds. Footsteps below, the irregular slap of a flip-flop. Jenn is surprised to see the hippie girl—the diver chick from the market—emerging from the olive grove. She is wearing a paint-stained man's vest, cinched at the waist with a belt made from rope, but even in rags, there's no disguising her beauty, the barely discernible bobbing of her breasts—no bra—and the tautness of her arms. Is this who they fought about last night? Jenn tries not to think on it, and instead focuses on the crone who is leaning over the balustrade to gawp at her as she passes below the terrace. She mutters to no one in particular and shakes her head—whether in admiration or approbation, Jenn can't be sure.

Sensing she's being watched, the girl looks up, makes the briefest eye contact with Jenn, and smiles smugly. She drives extra swagger into her walk, her young bum flipping beneath the flimsy fabric of the vest. Jenn watches her go. She drains the last dregs of orange juice, and as she sets down the glass, she appraises her own breasts. She has a deep cleavage—too big, she feels—but her breasts are still firm nevertheless and shapely for her age. Even the younger nursing-home workers are forever complimenting her on her figure—her tits, tits spared the ravages of suckling babies. The older girls never fail to get that one in whenever the young ones are complimenting her: "'Course, you haven't had kids, have you?"

If only they knew how that killed her.

Across the road, a van pulls up behind her car. A slender man in chef's uniform hops out and slides two huge trays from the back of the van, still hot, she judges, from his ginger grip, insulated by chunky towels. Jenn pays up, giggling out loud at the crone's disdain for the tip she leaves. She follows the man inside the shop.

The smells hit her in one delirious flush as she crosses the threshold: burned caramel and spice, then a salty, fish-infused aroma. Now if she could begin each morning with *that* rather than the choke of half-burned toast wafting out from the kitchen then she could withstand whatever trials the day might throw at her.

The young boy is hefting the pastries off the trays with a plastic spatula and carefully arranging them in the glass cabinet in front of the till. He indicates with a short, sharp glare, that the *diez minutos* has not yet elapsed. Jenn shrugs, prizes a copy of the *Sunday Times* out of the display, and bustles to the back of the tiny shop. Absentmindedly she fills a basket with things they might need for the walk: chips and nuts and water. She picks up a small bottle of olive oil and snorts at the price. This is the only grocery store in Deià and she wonders how the locals feel about the prices. Maybe they operate a two-tier system, with one price for residents and one for green, middle-class tourists like herself, ineffably beguiled by labels announcing their goods' "artisan provenance," all proudly—and expensively—*cultivada en Mallorca*. She retraces her steps along the aisles, matching the prices on the shelves with the things in her basket. Confounded at each turn, she returns each item until all that remains is the newspaper. She stows her red plastic basket, tucks the paper under her arm, and makes her way to the till. A small crowd has now gathered by the glass cabinet, ogling the tartlets and pastries. She chides herself for letting her mind wander. Nathan will be dry and dressed now, no doubt waking Emma with orange juice and coffee, sweet-talking her around from whatever quarrel they had last night.

Outside the village has shifted up a gear. Through the open door, Jenn can see the noses of two huge tourist coaches, sizing each other up from opposite ends of the village. Each steadily crawls toward the other. An impasse is inevitable—the buses are already creating a major backlog either way—but neither driver will back down. A man is hanging down from the café terrace where Jenn sat only minutes ago, capturing the face-off on his phone. Shit! Her car is stuck right in the middle of this debacle. Her plans of zipping up to the village and returning with breakfast are already in tatters—now she'll be lucky to get back before lunch . . . She's about to drop the paper and run when, finally, the kid favors her with the slightest nod of his head. She orders in Spanish—he replies in English. His blank face gives off an aloof insouciance: Please don't bother trying to interact, lady tourist. This is business. Give me money, then go. She's pleasantly surprised that it all comes to so little, and steps out with a paper bag laden with pastries and breads and tarts, their greasy warmth already soaking the paper with an oily sheen. She scurries back to the car, feels a momentary stab of relief that there's no parking ticket. The coaches have sorted out their differences and gone their separate ways. The village is busy but calm. She sets the pastry bag down firmly in the footwell and places the newspaper on the passenger seat. Only now does she realize she hasn't paid for it. It stayed tucked under her arm throughout the transaction and the uppity young lad didn't deign to inquire, and only now does she acknowledge that she knew exactly what she was doing. If he challenged her, she'd pay; if not, serves them right, the surly bastards! She starts the car, puts it in gear, heads off down the hill before indicating left and doubling back on herself; her heart is still thumping as she passes the little shop again. It's only as she turns off the main road and dips back down the beach track back toward the villa that the pounding gives way to the gentle thrill of having gotten away with it. There's a deeper joy, too. Within the hour, she will be serving Nathan—serving all of them— hot, sticky pastries up on the cliff. She passes a traffic warden, scootering back up the hill after nabbing some early birds at the beach. Jenn throws her a big cheery wave.

10.

The landscape has shifted. It's only a year since they last trekked the pine route to Sóller, but the familiar cliff path has been holed by a savage winter. It's completely blocked in places by fallen trees, some snapped at the waist, others uprooted entirely. Farther along, the cliff face has eroded so far into the headland as to take the path with it. The welcome piles of stones that for years have mapped out the way for walkers have been scattered and abandoned to the elements. Newly daubed bright red splotches on boulders and tree trunks direct them along a new route, away from the cliff face and high up into the hills through the darkest reaches of the forest. They push on, the mulch of decaying pine needles springy underfoot.

When they first started coming here, Jenn was able to convince Emma that the path pixies had laid down the stones especially for her and that, if followed diligently, they would lead her to treasure. They would hold hands, chattering all the way, Emma's excitable eyes scoping the forest for a pair of oval eyes or pointed ears peeping out from behind a trunk. Jenn smiles at the recollection of her diminutive, gap-toothed girl, grinning as she reached into a hollow to retrieve another treat wrapped in colored foil: a coin, a sweetie, sometimes a little book. Even when she was nine or ten, old enough to know otherwise, Emma still serviced the make-believe, affecting the same doe-eyed excitement each time they set off along the cliff path. And Jenn continued to set her alarm for the crack of dawn so she could sneak down to the woods in advance and lay out the trail of goodies. Now they hardly speak; now Emma walks on ahead with her arms folded tightly. The sight of it brings a sting to Jenn's eyes. Not quite nostalgia, nor even regret in this instance, but sadness at the passing of time. How wonderful those moments were. How quickly they moved on. Just like the weather, the cliff path.

Whatever the teenagers argued over last night still lingers in the air. Jenn thinks she's worked it out, and it's nothing more serious than opposed positions. The boy wants what the girl won't give; the girl won't give until the boy threatens to find it elsewhere—that's what yesterday's charade with the hippie girl was about. He was letting Emma know: If she won't, there's plenty who will. All the other girls do it, he'll be telling her. Jenn should tell her, too. Tell her how she was once that girl, holding out, holding it all in, hanging on to her virtue. How clever she'd thought herself back then. While her mates were upstairs chasing cheap thrills and cashing in their assets, she was downstairs saving for the future. When the time was right, she'd have her pick of the crop—and she'd have that option because she'd boxed clever. What she may have lacked in nubility she could more than make up for in nobility. *Her* boy would be able to hold his head high. No flies on Jenny O'Brien; she wasn't *one of those girls*. If only someone older and wiser had told *her*. Told her that, after a certain point in a woman's life, her past becomes open to reevaluation.

Once her flesh grows soft, once she gets married and has kids, once her allure dims, once that woman ceases to be a proposition, nobody cares *what you were* anyway. Nobody remembers. You exist to others only in relation to *what you became*—your husband, your kids, your job. All those missed opportunities. All those electrifying teenage encounters she'd denied herself, when her body was still young and firm. If she could have her time again, she wouldn't be so cautious, so damn clever. If she had her time again, Jenn O'Brien would bound up those stairs and unquestionably be *one of those girls*.

Nathan walks ahead with Gregory. They've bonded over football, it seems, discussing the pros and cons of Moyes as Manchester United's new manager. It still takes her by surprise to hear her husband pontificate on such laddish matters, but even there, he can't quite shake off his cap and gown. His didactic approach to what should be an easy, enjoyable conversation gives every impression that football—like modern art or Japanese film—is an educational topic rather than a passion.

Emma's eyes do not leave Nathan's back for one moment; his broad shoulders packed into an emerald-green polo shirt. He only has to turn his head a fraction and look in her general direction and Emma stands to attention, willing a smile from his lips: a look, a wave—any kind of peace offering. Jenn places a hand on Emma's shoulder, gives her a sympathetic squeeze.

"Everything okay there?"

"Yep."

The curt consonant is emphatic, a caveat. The matter is not open for discussion. Jenn is not giving up—not yet. She stops for full effect.

"The thing with boys, Em—" She sighs—she already knows how this will play, but she soldiers on. "What you should know about them is that they like to play—"

Emma spins around, exasperated. "Don't. You know nothing about him."

As well prepared as she thought she was, Jenn is taken aback by the venom of Emma's delivery, the anger in her eyes. She holds up her hands in surrender, smiles, tries not to betray her shock, her hurt. Only yesterday Emma was squeezing her fingers and thanking her for making this happen. Emma shakes her head, marches on in front. The gap between her teeth is still there.

❧

Suddenly the path just drops away. There is no indication in the landscape, no gradual descent or loosening of soil, nothing to suggest that the sudden slash of light and space is a sheer and deadly drop. They have walked this path many times before; they are respectful of the seasonal shifts of landscape, attentive to its ruses and hidden perils, yet it's Nathan, the novice, who spots it. Without warning, he shoots an arm across Gregory's chest.

"Whoa!"

Emma screams. A collective gasp followed by a prolonged silence. Perhaps if Emma hadn't snapped at her, Jenn might have realized they were climbing over a purposely erected barrier, not detritus; she might have noticed the daub of red some distance back, directing them up and away from the ledge. But none of them would have seen the warning sign that blew down in last week's gale. With both his trekking poles set firm in the soil, Gregory inches toward the edge. He cranes his head and shoulders forward to peer down; Jenn does the same. She swoons and quickly steps back. Just below the precipice, a tiny stone hut clings miserably to the clod of earth and rock that has simply plunged straight down into the gorge, carrying the little outhouse with it. The whole thing, edifice and the clump it stands on, is wedged halfway down the cliff. Below it there is nothing, no sea to break your fall, just boulders and fallen pines whose branches stand erect like rapiers.

Gregory turns to them, smirking.

"So this is how the municipality of Deià is keeping tourist saturation in check."

But there's fear in his eyes. He is thinking the same as everyone else: that could have been them. He backs away from the ledge, takes Emma's hand, and squeezes it tight. Only Nathan seems indifferent; he is already retracing their steps, trying to figure out where they went wrong.

"Here!" he shouts. "Eureka!" The splash of red paint on a rotted stump is inconclusive, they could veer left or right. Nathan points up to a farther flash of color in the trees above. "There we go. Problem solved."

Gregory doesn't move. "I don't know, guys . . . could be another bum steer."

Jenn cannot see that far up; Emma is not yet ready to take Nathan's side. He shrugs.

"Shouldn't we at least check it out?"

Emma bunches close to her father, who's still prodding the ground beneath his feet. Jenn shoots Nathan a sympathetic look, shrugs her approval. He smiles back and takes off into the woods. They follow his progress via splintered glimpses of emerald darting through the forest. The gradient is steep. He is right above the ravine now. It's a straight slide down to the precipice—loose soil all the way with little to grab hold of. If he were to slip, he could die.

"He's really high up," Emma says. She shuffles over, her grudge forgotten for a moment, and leans into Jenn's hip in search of succor. Jenn pulls her close.

"He's okay, Em. He knows what he's doing."

Greg tightens his lips, lets out a hiss. Jenn silences him with a look. Her bronchial passages are starting to tighten again. Her breathing drags, it feels woolen in her lungs. She casts her gaze out over the sea. The low clouds are lifting, patches of blue starting to break through. Yet she can feel it, is sure of it—a storm is on its way.

Nathan emerges in a clearing at the highest point of the forest. Here the trees thin out to meet the stepped terraces of an olive grove. They can just about make him out as he squats and rests his hands on his thighs. Then he's back up and off and out of sight again. Seconds later he's up in a clearing. He makes a beckoning gesture with his hand.

"Found it!" he shouts. "Come on!"

Gregory's face twitches. He mops a veil of sweat from his brow.

"We can't just cut through somebody's back garden," he says in a low voice. Nathan—fifty-odd meters above—calls back as though he's right there.

"It's not a garden—it's just an old olive grove."

He disappears from sight briefly, then reappears on the other side of the ravine, trotting down the slope like a goat. He's enjoying himself, smiling at them as he skips down to the cliff's edge as though it's all in a day's gentle work. Gregory's face tightens. He narrows his eyes and begins scanning around for an alternative way across the chasm. Jenn leans back on a tree trunk as he plots his own route. His lips move silently before, eventually, he reveals his master plan.

"Right. See back there where the mudslide leads down to the cove? Okay—follow it back. See the steps cut into the cliff face? That's the old path leading down to that little beach. Remember?"

She mentally traces his route down the side of the cliff. That little tier of footholds may well have functioned as steps at one time, but like the rest of the landscape they have crumbled beyond all recognition; no way are they stable.

"I don't know, Greg. You're the only one with proper walking shoes on. Why not scope out the other route."

She is careful not say *his* route. The roll of thunder turns their heads toward the sea. It's dense and guttural, as though coming from the very bowels of the ocean. Greg looks anxious for a moment; Jenn, vindicated.

"Did you bring your inhaler?"

"No. You predicted clear skies."

She lets him fret for a moment, then fishes the pink one from her pocket, takes a precautionary blast. Greg shouts across to Nathan, "You'll have to come back, Nathan! We're taking a different route. We need to press on."

Jenn tries to control her irritation. Once, she might have found Greg's obstinacy endearing; now she just sees it as folly. Nathan is standing there on safe, solid ground, shaking his head, and Jenn realizes in one furious flash that she's embarrassed for her husband, embarrassed *by* him. This bearded man with his hiking boots and collapsible trekking poles is a bad reflection on her. He drives the poles into the ground as he marches off, aloof. Emma scurries to catch him, grabs him by the wrist. With a stifled groan, Jenn pushes back against the tree with both palms, forcing herself forward.

"Greg! Don't you think we should at least *try* the other route? I mean, he's *there*, after all. He's on the other side!"

"The other side of *where* though? *This* is the path!" he shouts back. Jenn dawdles, unsure who to follow. The sky creaks and groans. Greg waves his stick at her.

"Jenn! Will you come *on?*"

She watches him scuff and slip his way up the slope, Emma almost dragging them both back down. She watches them until they're gone.

11.

The flea-bitten donkeys cease chewing as she comes sliding into the olive grove on her bottom. Cautiously she gets to her feet and skirts the curious beasts. She scans around for Nathan. He's straddling a fallen tree, making like he's looking out to sea but furtively observing her. He gets up, walks toward her, eases the rucksack from her shoulders, and swings it effortlessly over his.

"Is he always like that?"

There's a mocking glint in his eye. A defensive jolt shoots through her.

"Like what?"

He shrugs. "Childish. Stubborn."

She takes a step back.

"Greg knows the paths inside out. We've been walking here for years."

"What? Knows them well enough to put his daughter's life at risk?"

He strides toward the cliff ledge. Lightning rips the skyline. He points to the cove below and traces a path back from it with his finger.

"That's where he's heading to, down there?"

She follows his finger to the flimsy steps, which end abruptly halfway down the cliff. A landslide has left a bronze rubble scree sloping down to the rocky beach. Again a protective lurch, deep in her gut. She shrugs. "I'd imagine so. Who knows?"

"Madness," he mutters.

Even in the sheltered cove below them, the sea is rough, wild with bobbing gulls. There's the shimmer of a tin roof, a fisherman's shack. Small wooden boats strain at their moorings. Yes, she thinks, madness—and follows Nathan sideways, one foot planted carefully after the other, down the narrow path then slowly down the cliff steps.

There is no sand, no shingle, just boulders and rocks, stones and pebbles of various shapes and textures, some as smooth and huge as prehistoric eggs, others jagged enough to shred the soles of her feet. The stony cove is empty save for two women, one sitting between the other's legs, both staring out across the stormy sea. Jenn selects a rusty rock, wide and flat, just back from the water's edge. She squats and unpacks the food. Nathan narrows his eyes as he watches the older woman kiss her girlfriend's neck. Is that disapproval? Or is he, like most young men, beguiled? She taps his shoulder with a bottle of water. The face that greets her is neither leery nor judgmental—just wistful.

The sun comes out, yet rain spatters their shoulders. The sky bellows. Nathan does a sweep of the horizon.

"It's the mountain climate," she says. "Sometimes the sky can be pure blue, not a cloud ... and then, just like that, a downpour. Absolute torrents of rain. One summer we were sunbathing on the terrace, early June, then, next thing ..."

His body is twisted away from her, not listening, she thinks, not remotely interested in this middle-aged woman prattling on about family sojourns gone by. She stops mid-sentence, removes her shoes, closes her eyes, and lies back on the rock, her head turned away from him. She hopes Greg will be here soon.

"Listen!" he says. He gets to his feet, blocking the sun.

She sits up.

"Shhh," he says and holds up a finger. "Did you hear it?"

Greg is calling her name. It is coming from somewhere high above.

"Over there," he says.

He's pointing up the cliff face, way back down the coast. She can see them now, two squints of color at the top of the cliff. How did they get *there!* They are still on the wrong side of the ravine. Momentarily, she's vexed by his folly, but then he calls out again—*"Jenn!"*—and there's a desperate edge to his voice now. Nathan starts clambering back across the rocks. Jenn stumbles after him.

She can see them clearly, directly above, stuck on a ledge. Emma is lying sideways, crying.

"Come back!" Greg shouts. His voice echoes around the ravine. "She's broken her ankle."

"Oh for fuck's sake," Jenn mutters. Nathan shoots her a look. She shouts up to them, "Emma, darling. Can you stand?"

Emma tries to push herself up, screams, concedes defeat, and sits back down. Greg's red face comes leering down at them.

"Don't be fucking stupid! *Can she stand!* She's broken her ankle."

Jenn shakes her head at Nathan. "She won't have broken it. I bet you—just be a sprain."

"How come?"

"I know Emma."

And she does. She *knows* Emma: A girl predisposed to melodrama; a girl who cannot breathe unless she's the center of attention, who would rather let you run her to hospital than let you know the pain has subsided. With Emma a headache is always a migraine, a difference of opinion is always a fight. Once Jenn had stormed into school after Emma had rang her at work in floods of tears, claiming the sports teacher had forced her to play netball in her underwear. The reality, as it later transpired in the headmaster's office, was that Emma had forgotten her kit and the teacher had loaned her a pair of gym briefs, which, Jenn was forced to concede, were exactly the same as the blue nylon ones she happily donned for cross-country. Nathan looks at her, surprised. Jenn finds herself wondering whether he'll snitch on Emma's uncaring, disbelieving stepmother. Right now she doesn't give a shit.

"I'm taking her back," Greg shouts. "Got to get this looked at."

He scoops his daughter up in his arms. There's a martyred tone to his voice and it is underscored by accusatory sub-notes. Somehow this has become Jenn's doing: If only she'd taken *his* route, if only she hadn't defied him, she'd be there to attend to Emma.

She doesn't have to say a word to Nathan. They begin packing up the plastic plates and food, the picnic futile now. The two women are frolicking in the sea. The wind is whipping cold, and the waves are buffeting them this way and that, but they are laughing, fearless, absolutely lost to the moment.

Jenn shifts herself around to watch them, vicariously enjoying the spray and tug of the water, the sense of liberation that comes from being out there, in the wild open sea. That would have been her, once upon a time; she would have been first in, and she'd have swum way, way out.

She stands up on the rock. At first, she isn't sure she's going to do this. She eases her arms out of her vest then suddenly, speedily, begins to undress; she delves into the rucksack for her swimsuit and disappears behind a boulder.

"What are you doing?"

"Going for a swim."

"Now?"

She emerges in her bikini—no fussy swimsuit for Jenn today. His eyes roll across her, up and down.

"Shouldn't we head back?"

"You can, if you want."

She scrambles across the rocks and lets her momentum take her headlong into the sea, grazing her knee on a reef as she kicks out. It's even colder than yesterday, but she's taken over, immediately and completely, by a monumental onrush of well-being. Every few strokes the thermal changes—fresh, freezing, bracing—but the slap of the sea on her skin is divine. She pauses, swirls salt water around her mouth and spits it out, ready to take on the might of the ocean. Only her battered lungs protest.

She rests up on her back, the waves stinging her cheeks as she lets the swell take her weight. She cranes her head back awkwardly to view the crag, careful this time not to drift too far from the shoreline. Nathan has gone. She feels a stab of betrayal, quickly eclipsed by a pervading exasperation—at him, at the whole bloody thing, the way their holiday has been derailed. This will not happen again, she pledges. Next year, she and Greg will come away together. Alone. End of story.

She can sense the rain before it falls. A heavy gauze hangs above the sea. She strikes back for the shore. Fat, solid raindrops pelt her scalp—then comes the downpour, just like she'd told him, just like that. She pushes harder, her arms heavy, numbed by the cold. The cove is in sight, but she's viewing it through a blurred and streaky lens. Her foot trails and scrapes hard against a rock. It's uneven, but she can stand, just—and from there she can launch herself across to another submerged ledge. The swell knocks her back into the sea, and she has to use all her upper-body strength to clamber back onto the rock. She catches her breath, then wades the final few meters to the shoreline. Once she's in the shallows, she has to sit until her heartbeat slows. It takes her three determined efforts to haul herself out of the water. She sits on the serrated edge of a rock, shivering as she struggles to catch her breath. The rain is dancing off the sea.

The towel is placed across her shoulders with such tenderness and care that, for a second, she thinks the women have come to her rescue, but the arm that gently helps her up is thick and manly. She takes his hand and allows herself to be pulled to her feet. She stays close to him as the rain slams down in sheets and the slick rocks turn slippery.

There is a hollow in the cliff face no more than four or five meters deep and just high enough to stand.

"You're shivering," he says. "You need your inhaler?"

A ripple of anxiety beneath the skin. This is no time to be vulnerable. She takes the towel and rubs her hair, vigorously. He drops to his knees, rifles through the rucksack. Functioning now, she takes the rucksack from him, delves for her inhaler. She drags on it and leans against the dank limestone, waiting for her airways to stretch open again. Nathan stands back, a bemused smile playing on the corners of his mouth.

"You're mad, you."

She ducks away from his gaze, fishes in the rucksack, brings out two paper bags, passes one to him. She squats against the wall, and he hunkers down next to her. She eats hungrily, without restraint or embarrassment. The starchy inner flesh of the pastries has cooled and solidified, smearing her fingers in orange grease. The explosion of flavors, one after another—spinach and anchovies and olive oil—is good, each mouthful restoring her.

The thunder rumbles again, closer, directly above them, lifting Nathan's eyes to the roof of the cave—and then onto her. The air is fat and tight. Their knees keep touching in the darkness. There can be no room for ambiguity here. She stands and shuffles to the back of the hollow with her clothes. She squats down among the rubble of beer cans and papers and the charred remains of a campfire. Outside the rain slams down harder, bouncing high off the rocks and starting, now, to flood into the cave. Jenn puts on her trainers and swings the rucksack onto her back. She leans back against the cave wall, using the rucksack as a buffer. In the half-light, she can feel Nathan's gaze seeking her out. She fixes her eyes outside, following the rolling clouds with a studied super-concentration. The rain abates as suddenly as it came. She drops the rucksack, moves to the mouth of the cave. There is an aura of silver brightness pushing at the horizon. Though her chest dictates they should sit it out a while longer, common sense urges her to press on.

"Rain's cleared." She squints. "We should make tracks

while we can . . ." She turns—he is just standing there, dead still, staring at her, with his hands hanging down by his slender hips. His expression is intense, his eyes slowly picking over her ribs, one by one, all the way up to her face, his eyes on hers. When she can stand it no longer she ducks back into the hollow and passes around him to grab the rucksack. The moment they draw level, his hand reaches out to grab her wrist. He moves his fingers down over her palm and slots them through hers. She can't look at him. She stands there, letting him stroke her hand, staring out to sea; he is looking back into the cave. His touch feels like hot, wet earth. Her breathing is staccato, too loud. It fills the entire cave. Gently, firmly, she untwines her fingers from his. She stumbles out of the cave, climbs down over rocks and away. She grapples her way up the scree slope. She doesn't look back.

12.

Her heart sinks when she reaches the top of the dirt track. Benni's white van is in the driveway; their rented car is nowhere to be seen. Benni is perched on a small ladder, picking the last of the lemons. At the creak of the gate he swivels, almost overbalancing in his eagerness. He comes down the ladder, smiling. Jenn increases her pace over the last few yards and bounds up the front steps. She can feel Benni hard on her heels.

"Tomorrow I ask Maria to make you the most spectacular lemon tart. A gift from us."

He's talking to her as he holds up the basket of lemons, but his eyes are fixed on Nathan. The tart is just a smoke screen, a subterfuge. Jenn doubts it will ever materialize. He nods at Nathan—she does not introduce them.

"That's very kind of you," she says, then turns away from him and opens the door.

"I see you have new guest. I don't think I have met, have we?"

"Nathan, Benni; Benni, Nathan." She ushers Nathan

across the threshold, gives Benni a valedictory smile, and resolutely shuts the door.

He leans back against the oak frame as he flips off his sodden trainers. For one moment her gaze rests on the light ripple of muscle beneath his soaking T-shirt. She can't bear it, can't bear him. She turns and walks.

Upstairs she locates her phone, still attached to its charger that is hot to the touch. She dials. Gregory's phone rings out from downstairs. She dials Emma's, it runs on to voice mail. When she comes back down, Nathan is sprawled across the settee in his boxers. His wet clothes are strewn across the backs of chairs. He is leaving Emma a message. Jenn hangs on to the bottom spindle of the stairway.

"Can't get through," he says. "Fancy a coffee?"

As though nothing happened back there. As though the silence they endured all the way back, the contrived distance they maintained, right to the bottom of the dirt track, was completely normal. Perhaps it didn't happen. Perhaps this is all in her head.

He goes through to the kitchen, snaps on the kettle. She stands at the patio doors, stares out across the pool, wondering if she should bite the bullet and ask Benni to drive her up to the hospital. The sky is blackening over once again, the distant rumble of thunder. The kettle is whistling. Benni moves into focus among the trees, raking bruised lemons into a pile. His eyes keep darting across in shifty, sidelong glances. No way can she ask for his help. Gregory is right to dislike the obnoxious old pest. Why does he keep turning up like this, day after day? There's always some excuse—he's picking fruit or he's cleaning the pool. It's his house, of course, he owns the place, but for these two weeks it is *theirs*. Yesterday he was here when they got back from Valldemossa. They watched him from the kitchen, ogling Emma sunbathing by the pool. Greg was ready to march outside and have it out with him, but she'd stopped him. Joked, bitterly, that he had no qualms about Benni seeing his wife in her bikini. Next time her husband threatens to chase him, she will not stand in his way. The next time her husband asks her to do something, she will do it. She is deeply sorry; she wants him home. She wants everything back to normal.

She moves away from the patio doors, hovers at the bottom of the stairs. Hears the suck of steam as the kettle is upended into the French press. A little wince of pain as the plunger, shoved down in haste, squirts hot coffee onto his hands. Strong, masculine hands; soft, slender fingers. Her stomach lurches.

He comes into the room, sips at a mug of coffee.

"There's plenty in the pot if you change your mind."

As though he were talking to his flatmate. His dad. He slumps down on the sofa, puts his legs up on the table, picks up his iPad, and starts typing with both hands. What is he writing? What is he saying?

"Going for a shower," she says. "Can you try Emma again?"

He doesn't even dignify the request with a nod. She peers down as she goes by; he's almost filled up the page.

Upstairs she locks the bedroom door, then the bathroom door. Turns on the shower—as hot as she can bear it. She soaps and soaks the loofah and sets about sloughing off the salt, the sea, everything from her skin. His skin touching hers. A stabbing within. She removes the showerhead from its hook, directs the water spray between her legs. Gasps at the shock of the touch, the alien sensation radiating out from deep within. A hot, scratchy sound in her throat as she drags the showerhead up and down, once, twice, its length, its hardness too much to bear. She stops. Latches the showerhead back onto the wall. Gets out. Wipes the steam from the mirror to observe herself, to chide herself. She traces a finger along the soft dimpled flesh of her thighs and buttocks, touches the tired appendix scar, cups her hopeless breasts—squeezes them together then lets them drop. Still that urgency, the pulsing throbs between her thighs.

She is surprised to hear music coming from his room— "Unravel" by Bjork, an all-time favorite track. Could he possibly know that? Of course not. Why is he playing it so loud? What message is he sending her? None. Nothing. Drive this folly out. She dries, dresses, creeps past the door, wanting to get downstairs, get as far away as possible. The door is half open. An invitation. The thought intoxicates her. She crushes it, steps quickly past, and strides downstairs.

She goes into the kitchen. Busies herself. The rain has stopped. A wind shaking the lemon grove, overripe fruit dropping from the trees. She hears a couple of mopeds whining back up the hill. She ventures outside to hang the wet clothes. Benni is loading up his van. She comes back in. Just the two of them. Is this what she wanted? No. No. He is in the lounge now. She goes upstairs and puts away the washing. She lies flat out on the bed. She can't settle, can't find peace to do anything.

Downstairs.

She is in the kitchen, reading *Walden*, the same sentence over and over, taking none of it in. He walks in and pours a glass of water, lingering long enough for her to take in his hard young body. Impossible. Unfair. Fuck you, she thinks. Fuck Emma. She turns away, goes back to her book.

He comes over. Places the glass of water on the table in front of her, forcing her to look up at him.

"What?" she snaps.

She slaps shut her book, gets up, the chair scraping the floor, an unceremonious screeching, a rebuttal. He follows her through the archway into the lounge. His hands are at her waist, pushing her up against the wall, the prow of his dick digging into her buttocks. He sucks her shoulder. Lifts the hair from her neck. She keeps her eyes trained to the white-washed wall in front, will not look at him. Maddened by his audacity, devastated when he pulls away.

"Jenn," he says.

She will not look, and as long as she doesn't look, as long as she keeps staring at the wall, this is not happening.

The flat of his palm between her legs. She parts them slightly—but she does not spread them, she does not give in. He works her with three fingers; he is holding the entire weight of her body in his hand as he grips and lifts. Her pulse beats in his hand. The sound of the car coming up the dirt track. She rolls back and forth on his hand, clenching, trying to goad him with her buttocks, pleading with him to finish her off. His hand stays dead still.

"Kiss me," he says, breathing into her shoulder. The car turns into the driveway. He increases the pressure of his hand but it remains fixed, like a clasp, keeping her stitched up, held together. Still in control, but how badly she wants to let go. A yelp seems to rear up from her guts. It is not release or ecstasy but mercy, soaking through her pants to meet the sweat-hot cradle of his palm. The slap of a car door. Only one. Where is

Emma? Footsteps on the terrace. His hand drops away, leaving her wide open, bereft. The cool sweep of the air-conditioning breezes across the damp of her face, her soaking briefs. He hastens to the couch, picks up her book. She is still standing in the archway, dazed, when Gregory comes in. He is carrying Emma and her leg is in plaster.

13.

Jenn watches daybreak from the kitchen window; streaks of green and pink slowly scratch the sky to life. The sea begins to glint, turning from gray to rippling silver. Not wanting to wake the house with the rumble of the electric kettle, she boils a pan of water on the stove. The French press is clogged with yesterday's coffee and she just cannot be bothered. She digs out a jar of instant from the back of the cupboard. She has to stab the hardened coffee granules with a knife, then scrape it out. She lifts the pan from the stove; it keeps up its faint, melancholy bubbling and she pours water into the cup. She drinks the coffee black, no sugar, recoiling at the first tentative sip, dirty and bitter like the residue of last night's dreams. She swigs more, gulps hard. It scours her throat and feels right somehow; it feels like sacrament.

❧

She has no concept of time, no idea how long she has stood at the window—but the coffee is cold, and outside a mound of split and withered lemons is now visible in the pale morning light, raked into a compost pile at the farthest corner of the grove. Her mind loops: every train and twist of thought goes back to him. She places a hand on her chest; her heart skulks low in its cage. She would like to take it out and run it under the cold tap; she would like to wash away the grease and rawness until the juices run clear. She would like to march right up to his room and ask him to leave. She's rehearsed the moment enough, these past few hours. But whenever she steels herself to the possibility, she is floored by the outcome. She pictures him gone, and she starts to come undone.

She goes out to the terrace, the fresh morning light picking out the shabbiness of the recliners. The decking is dirty, its weatherproofing beginning to peel underfoot. Gingerly, she lowers herself onto one of the chairs. Its cushioned padding is damp. Her eyeballs throb. She can feel her dull pulse through her eye sockets. It's a long time since she's felt this sleep-starved. She sits a while, drifting, thinking back to the night shifts at the nursing home, all those years ago. Twelve-hour shifts, sometimes ten days in a row. If she could make the 7:30 a.m. bus back to Rochdale, she might be able to get four hours kip in, before her afternoon stint at the bookies'. Greg put a stop to all that. He put a stop to a lot of things—for the better. Within six months of meeting him, she'd handed in her notice, gone back to college, and inherited a daughter. Five years later she was managing a nursing home. She listened to him back then; she trusted him. Greg always seemed to know what was right for her and how to make it happen. She'd never had that before—not from any of her teachers and certainly not from any boyfriend. Her dad had always shown faith in her, but that was different. His was more of a blind belief in her ability to make a go of things—to make the best of a bad hand. And she did; she was a grafter, Jenn. She was a worker, and she got herself out there, earning a living and living the life, after a fashion. *You're a grafter, aye, love. Just like your mam.* He's there for a moment; she could reach out and touch him, until she blinks. Dad. What would he make of her now? He was very fond of "Grigree." It didn't matter that he was older, or that he was the father to a baby girl. He was good; a good solid man with a good job and a good solid name. Grigree. He had a good solid look too. Everything about him was big and commanding, reassuring. The sort of man a father wants for his daughter.

Ж

There's a crunch like the crushing of salt in a grinder as she tips her neck forward. Her shoulders hurt from sleeping in the spare bed last night, little more than a flimsy mattress on its hewn rock base. Once upon a time it had been a treat for Emma to be allowed to sleep down there. She'd never dream of it now.

At one point she thought she heard footsteps. Whoever it was seemed to linger outside her door before shuffling back up the stairs. Greg? Had he come to apologize? He'd been cool with her since he got back from the hospital, and even though he didn't say it, because he knew how unfair—how absurd—it might sound, deep down he blamed her for the accident on the cliff. She'd felt him stewing away in bed, simmering in the darkness. His eyes were closed but she could feel his mind ticking over, laying down his resentment—his vindication—between them like an unwelcome guest. When he did finally drift off, she was unable to. She took her featherless pillow and went downstairs. The footsteps outside the door were faltering, nervous, too light for Greg's. But she couldn't know. And once the thought had invaded—the possibility that Nathan had come to her in the night, eager to slip between her sheets—there was no getting back to sleep. That wasn't much more than a couple of hours ago. Now the sun is on the rise, already starting to disperse the low bank of clouds that mottle the tips of the mountains. She can hear a van chugging down the hillside. And somewhere, on the other side of the hill, goat bells announce the new day. She is not ready for it, not yet. She picks up her chair and takes herself around to the side of the house. It's shady here, cooler; the grass is still damp. She closes her eyes and tries to forget.

✠

She's aware of the creak of the gate, but she cannot drag herself awake. Then come the sighs and the panting for breath, macho sounds of exhaustion, recuperation. He hasn't seen her up there, in the shadow. He's bent double, his palms on his knees, catching his breath. He straightens and comes limping up the path, stiff-legged, his T-shirt pulled over his head like a kaffiyeh. The rutted ridges of muscle on his rib cage are speckled with beads of sweat. He slurps water from the standpipe, splashes his face, and slumps back against the wall; and she feels it like a kick in the guts. Greg had a dozen more eloquent ways of describing the depravity of that sensation. He'd written most of them in the mist of the bathroom mirror when they first started screwing—one each morning for weeks, and she'd thought they were his. But whomever he was quoting—Shelley or Coleridge—none of them got as close as the clichés did to the naked savagery of that primal passion. Seeing Nathan was like being hit by a truck; she is seeing stars; it is gut-wrenching.

He's been running. His shorts are saturated. When did he slip out? Why didn't she see him? Did *he* see *her*? He hauls himself over the little wall. As his shorts strain, she can see the outline of his cock. He pads across the terrace like a puma, then he's gone. Out of sight. She can hear the squeak of his sweaty palm on the doorjamb as he supports himself with one hand and flips off his trainers with the other.

There's a prolonged silence as she waits to hear his footsteps. He must have gone up to his room. The voice takes her by surprise.

"You didn't sleep either, then?"

It seems to be coming from directly above her, from the kitchen window. She doesn't stir. Concentrates on a sandy gecko astride the rim of a chunky terra-cotta pot.

"Jenn? Can we talk?"

She cannot say the words. He runs the tap. She hears him sighing as he fills a glass. She pictures the undulations in his throat as he slakes his raging thirst, and her stomach folds in on itself. The glass is set down firmly. She hears it hit the table with a decisive thud. She's thinking it all out, preparing her big speech when he comes back over the terrace. He seems to flicker in and out of vision, like a film reel—he's there, yet he is not real. She knows what she has to say; it must be good and it must be final.

As though he's read her eyes and knows his fate, Nathan turns sharply, stops with his back to her, and hesitates, his shoulders rising and falling. He starts to say something then strangles it, strides back inside the villa. Minutes later, she hears the shower in the main bathroom being powered up. She feels vulnerable, rejected. She heads inside to find him but steadies herself, lingers in the kitchen, thinking, thinking. She puts the kettle on for coffee.

He is sitting in his underpants at the desk in the bedroom, deep in thought, deep in flow, his pen moving deftly across the page. It takes a moment for her eyes to adjust and the image takes her by surprise—although it shouldn't. There was a time, not so long ago, when barely a morning went by without her coming down to find him this way, hunched over the kitchen table, hammering the keys of his clunky old typewriter. He told her, back then, that it made him feel more like a writer—the travail of banging away on his Olympia. But that last batch of rejections seemed to snuff out Greg's flame for good.

He still wrote—but he wrote to order, not for himself. He wrote articles for journals; he wrote about the forgotten women poets of the Romantic era, Hemans and Landon. Who even cares about this stuff, he'd say, booting up his laptop with a weary resignation as she was turning in for the night. But right now she knows it's not a Romantic driving his motor. He is working on something of his own. Something new perhaps—she knows better than to ask. She pauses at the door to watch him for a while. His forearms and neck are red-brown, but his torso is white. The sight of him stirs pity in her—a new ingredient in their relationship, and one she doesn't like.

His pen hovers as he registers her presence, before diving

back to the page with renewed alacrity. She tiptoes over and sets the tray down to the side of him. He pauses to take in the coffeepot, freshly made lemonade, and yesterday's pastry, revived in the oven. He's aware of what this is, a peace offering, and he takes her wrist and squeezes it, kisses it—then he takes up his pen again.

"Somewhere there's beauty; somewhere there's freedom; somewhere he is wearing his white flower," he says.

"Beautiful."

"Isn't it? If only it were mine."

She hovers, hoping he'll elaborate, but he turns back to the page, twirling the pen between his fingertips. She lays a gentle hand on his shoulder, leaves him to it.

❦

She runs a bath. She tips in a miniature bottle of rose-hip bubble bath. She's going to lie back and close her eyes for ten minutes, and when she opens them she will start anew. She can draw a line and move forward. She smiles, happy-sad, as she bins the Malmaison bottle and remembers their night in Edinburgh. Their tenth wedding anniversary. On impulse she'd bought a wine-colored basque and matching suspender belt from a lingerie boutique on the High Street, but Greg was uneasy; he hadn't wanted her "trussed up." She felt foolish as she took the unwanted underwear back the next day, still in the plastic bag with the labels intact. She took him for lunch with the refund. She still felt foolish as she ordered a bottle of burgundy she knew he'd adore but could never afford.

The bubbles are spilling over the side and she snaps the taps off. When she slides in, water sloshes onto the floor. For a moment, silence. Calm. The peace is broken by Greg calling out to Emma that he'll be with her in a moment. She hears the grudging scrape of his chair, the slap of his feet as he huffs past the door and turns into the corridor. Is he talking to Nathan out there? She strains an ear through the rumble of the pipes. She can hear his nervous laughter, see his dimple as he smiles and tries to please. His white, even teeth. She squeezes her thighs tight together, and how quickly her resolve and regret turns to hunger.

She ducks her whole head beneath the water and tries to wrench herself free of him, dampen her thoughts with the mundane. When did Greg say they were replacing Emma's temporary plaster? Do they have to return the crutches? Does she need to give their bank a call to check whether the travel insurance that comes with their premium account has excesses or exclusions? It's useless. The smarting between her legs is painful now, impossible to ignore. She should attend to it before it takes over.

Uneasy with the feel of her fingers, she slides the soap bar between her legs. It slips away; she has to dig her nails in to get some purchase. Slowly she eases it to the spot where the ball of his hand had held her, his for the taking. She moves the bar gently, down then up, down then up, tentatively at first, out of synch with her accelerating heartbeat. Down then up, again and again, until she is no longer conscious of the act itself; she is looking down on her oscillating wrist slamming in and out. Bathwater slaps onto the floor in rhythmic waves. Jenn lifts her hips, her face screwed up, her eyes shut tight to the whitewashed wall of the archway, just down there. Yesterday. She fills herself with the feel of his hands on her waist, the veins pumped up on his wrists as he felt for her, lifted her up.

And the smell of him, the salty damp in his hair, his sweat, so complex in all its notes, all of which mingle to conjure the smell of youth. She stops. Her wrist is numb from squeezing the soap so hard. A few more strokes and she'll be gone, but with it, he is gone, too—and she can't bear that. She wants to hold on to it—to him—as long as she can. She wants to turn herself right around and kiss him, like he asked her to. She wants to kiss him hard, on the mouth. And then. And then she'll let him go.

"Jenn! For God's sake, open the door!"

She stiffens, drops the soap. The voice comes again.

"What's the matter?"

She can hear it in her voice, the automatic, overly gay cadence of a child who's been caught with a biscuit before tea.

"You've locked the door," he says. Not a question but a statement. He shakes the handle for emphasis.

"Jesus, Greg—just use the main bathroom."

She is no longer squirming but indignant. Irate.

"I need to speak with you."

The angry ball of heat moves up from her thighs to her stomach and continues to thud as she steps out of the bath and pads to the door, her wet hair dripping a trail behind her.

She pauses before she undoes the catch. She feels exposed, found out. It's obvious what she's been doing, what she's been thinking. She winces at the telltale red of her cheeks. She swoops for a towel, dabs between her thighs, and drapes it around her. A pulse in her neck beats fast as she slides back the lock and wonders: *Did he tell her, then?* Has Nathan told Emma? Even if not, is this how it will be from now on? Every raised voice, every question or silence met with *is this it?* Greg pushes his way in.

"It's Emma," he says. He presses his lips together, tries a smile; if anything, he looks embarrassed. "Can you give her a hand? She needs a bath."

Her relief at this stay of execution is quickly overtaken by ire. Does he not even suspect? Is it beyond his imagination that a young, beautiful male might desire his ageing wife? She slips into a toweling robe. Her voice comes out as a rasp, dry and brittle.

"So do I! Couldn't you or Nathan sort it out between you?"

A breeze from the balcony drifts across her Judas cheeks. She puts a hand to her face, still hot to the touch.

A streak of anger snaps in his expression. "Nathan? You think that's appropriate? You'd be okay with him seeing our daughter naked?"

No. I wouldn't, she thinks, and a zip slides down, opening her up, her nerve endings raw and exposed. Greg bends from the waist to retrieve the bar of soap from the floor and places it back in the soap dish. Without any further deference to her, he sheds his underpants and steps into the bath.

"Oh yes! Nice . . ." He lowers himself, releases the plug to let out some of the water. "I was thinking we might drive up to Sóller later, seeing as we didn't quite make it yesterday. What d'you reckon? Nice lunch at the Gran Hotel?" He immerses himself fully beneath the bubbles. She hears him pop up again. "The number's on the corkboard if you fancy giving them a ring."

She pictures him wiping the suds from his eyes, a foamy hat on his head, looking a tiny bit baffled and a tiny bit betrayed as he registers the empty room.

He is there in the corridor, standing barefoot on one

of the chintzy pews. He is on his tiptoes, his upper body
wedged in the small, circular window as he leans out trying to
reach something; she tries not to stare at the taut brown back
exposed as his T-shirt rides up. She keeps her gaze trained on
Emma's door as she draws level with the pew. Suddenly, with
a deft jump, he's down again, next to her. His hands are carefully cupped.

"Look."

He opens them tentatively, like a book he doesn't want
you to read. Sheltered in the cup of his palm is a little gecko.
It limbers up on its front legs as though trying to get a proper
look at her.

"He likes you."

The space behind the creature's front leg is pulsing wildly.

"It's terrified," she says. He closes his hand around it and
half turns his body from her, as though the critter were a toy,
and she might snatch it away.

"No—he just senses your fear," he says. "He's responding
to your pulse. Once you slow down, he will, too."

They stand there like that for a while, understanding
everything, saying nothing. She doesn't flinch when his big
toe presses down lightly on her foot. Encouraged, he moves
across to stroke the roof of her instep. She drops her chin
to watch his beautiful brown toe move around to probe the
queasy hollow of her ankle.

He ducks his face down to meet hers, and still holding
the creature, he tips her chin up with the tip of his thumb and
moves his lips toward hers. She closes her eyes for one second,
willing it to happen, before turning sharply away and stretching her neck so she's looking right through him into Emma's
room. The door is open.

"No."

She brings her head back around to face him. His eyes seek her.

"Yes," he says. "Please."

She gulps. It hurts.

"Once," she whispers. "Then we go back." Her breathing is staccato. She swallows hard, fighting to control her pitch and timbre. "Yes? We go back to how it was before." He nods. She takes a step back and away from him. He kneels and releases the lizard onto the balcony. He stays where he is, squatting, staring at the waxed floor.

Jenn steps toward him; stands over him. She loosens the belt, slips her bathrobe open. He lifts his chin, rests his head against her thigh. She is still swollen and he finds her easy enough. Her thighs are trembling slightly and he grips her buttocks to steady her. His tongue is measured and precise.

She is aware of Gregory humming on the other side of the wall, a plug being pulled, and a little way behind her, their daughter making her frustration known.

She rocks with him, muttering and whimpering. Weightless. Her whole body lifted, cut adrift and yet anchored firmly to his mouth. A tenuous, tingling thread. And her legs give way so she becomes the thread. She can feel it approaching, a gentle burr like the rail tracks before the train approaches, intensifying; and she can taste the metal of the tracks in her mouth as his tongue pushes her to the edge.

He pulls away, and it is so sudden, so cruel that she almost lashes out. He gets to his feet. There's just a sliver of space between them as she stands there, panting, hanging wide open. She tries to make eye contact, pleading with him to finish her off, but he will not look at her. There's no semblance of dignity now—she doesn't care what he thinks. She just wants it, this, purged from her body.

"Do you want me to beg? Is that what you want?"

He shakes his head, tucks a piece of hair behind her ears tenderly. His hand reaches down between her legs, cupping her, holding her in, stopping her from falling apart right there in front of him. She groans loudly and pushes herself down into his hand and tries to wriggle against it but he pulls away. He stands up, pulls down his shorts.

"Look."

She closes her eyes. Shakes her head.

"We can't," she begins. His mouth is on hers; his tongue is jabbing around her gums, the wrinkled roof of her mouth. He pulls away a second time.

"Look at me," he says.

She looks him in the eye. She reaches out and cups his balls and squeezes gently. Nathan closes his eyes, bites his lip. Then he steps into her, furious. And when it hits her, it slams her hard and fast, as life once had.

※

She's steeling herself for some kind of rebuke as she secures the belt of her dressing gown in a knot and taps meekly on Emma's door, but in the stretch of silence that follows, Jenn is no longer sure. Her pulse soars. Her fate drags through her: Emma saw them. She's drowned herself.

The voice that calls her in is shy and unsuspecting, and Jenn lingers outside the en suite and waits for her pulse to slow. On the other side of the wall she can hear the scrape of Greg's chair as he settles at the desk once again; and from

Nathan's room, music: some plaintive Middle Eastern melody played out over a techno drum beat. The villa resumes its proverbial rhythm. She pushes open the door.

Emma is sitting in the bath, the plastered ankle elevated on the ledge. The water has almost drained.

"I've washed myself," she says. "Just need some help getting out."

She is bashful in her nakedness, her arms folded across her breasts like a pair of bat's wings and, not for the first time, Jenn is struck by how much, and how quickly, their relationship has altered. It wasn't that long ago that Emma would sail into their bathroom, usually without knocking, and take a shower while Jenn was in the bath. Sometimes she'd wander in just to chat. She'd perch on the toilet with her knees tucked under her chin, or she'd sit on the lip of the bathtub and dangle her feet in.

She should have been better prepared. Jenn's friends never tired of discussing the dreaded teens, and they joked how adolescence had made monsters of their delightful children, but when it happened to Emma, she struggled. Jenn could never quite grant her the same level of understanding and sympathy that her friends did their spiky teens. They seemed to buzz off it, forever trying to best one another over whose child had committed the most despicable crime, and they'd serve up their anecdotes with a sprinkling of amusement, a flash of pride. Jenn didn't get it. There was nothing intriguing about Emma's mood swings, nothing funny about the way she spoke to her these days. It was sad and hurtful. After everything Jenn had done, everything Jenn had given up. It felt like a betrayal.

"So how are we going to do this? Let's see . . ." Jenn makes a conscious effort to twist her face away from Emma's body as she leans forward and slips an arm beneath her armpit. "Put your right hand around the top of my back." She bends from the knees and takes the weight of her with her hips, like she was taught before hoists became compulsory. But Jenn is out of practice: It's been a long time since she manually lifted a patient, and she can't quite lever her upward from this awkward angle. She releases her grip and lowers Emma back into the bath. Emma's breasts are exposed for a moment. Their womanly fullness, contrasted with Emma's childlike coyness, brings Jenn close to tears.

She looks away and tries again. "Ow! Ow"—and fails. "Sorry, Em. Bit out of practice."

"Well remind me to stay clear of whichever nursing home you're in charge of when I'm a decrepit old cow."

Jenn draws herself upright and laughs. She places her hands on her lower back and digs deep with her thumbs. For a few fleeting seconds, what happened out there on the landing—didn't. She's here, immersed in the moment, enjoying this rare episode of levity with her daughter.

Emma extends her hands, impatient now. "Come on, it's not like Health and Safety are watching. Just pull me out."

Jenn nods. She's aware of her own heavy breathing, lifting her chest, a solid choke of shame in her throat as she takes her daughter's hands and hauls her up.

She sits on the bed and towel-dries Emma's hair. Rubs sun cream into her shoulders. She's drawn to a beauty spot, the size of pinprick, on the back of her neck. She can't help but think: Does he know it exists? Does he kiss it? Where else does he kiss? She will not dignify these thoughts. At the other end of the corridor, he turns up his music. Greg slams their bedroom door. Jenn's eyes go back to the beauty spot. Back to the landing. It happened. No going back. Her brain is boiling. She cannot cool it down. She has to get out. She helps Emma into her shorts and makes her excuses.

She lies back on the lounger. She can hear laughter from down in the *cala*. The incessant slap of flip-flops on the beach road. The gecko is there on the patio; it freezes for a moment and pins her with its globular eyes. What? You saw nothing. It zips along the edge of the pool, disappears into the scrub. Upstairs Greg is closing the shutters. The music has stopped. Under the glare of the sun, none of it seems real.

14.

"Never really seen the point of the guided tour," Greg says, gesturing to the coachload of tourists inching past on the hairpin bend. "I mean you only truly know a place if you discover it for yourself."

They are ten minutes into their journey to Sóller and the car's puny air-conditioning has yet to kick in. The air is dense and suffocating, yet Greg is still insistent that the air-con will start to function any minute; he's asked them to keep the windows up.

Jenn lowers her face to the air vents. A wheeze of something lukewarm wafts out across her chin. Exasperated, she winds down the window. Greg mumbles, "Thanks for that." She pretends not to hear. The rush of cool air on her cheeks is gorgeous. She dangles an arm out, sweeping the roof of the pine forests and the sea with the tips of her fingers. She can taste the ocean. Greg gives up and winds down his window, too. She tilts her head out and trains her eyes on the sea. The road twists and dips through the headland.

They hear the surge of the accelerator before they turn the hairpin bend and almost run into the back of it: a white Citroen van, splayed across the middle of the road. The driver is revving the engine, struggling against the incline. Boxes and suitcases have been stacked haphazardly onto its roof. A skinny girl in denim shorts stands with her back to them, directing the driver through his side mirror. Greg slows to a stop behind the van. He clicks his tongue, slaps his thigh with one hand. Jenn shares his frustration. The stalled jalopy is falling to bits—the rear bumper has come away on one side, and the exhaust rattles and judders as it pumps a flume of dark gray smoke into the mountain air. On the other side of the van, in the oncoming direction, a line of cars and coaches is starting to build and this, in turn, is fusing yet more panic into the driver's thinking. He revs again, inching forward minutely before slamming on the hand break as the van's tires smolder and it slips back again. The girl slaps the van's back doors hard, warning the driver to brake. She goes around to the front of the van, shaking her head. The driver revs again. The jalopy lurches forward, rolls back.

"Are they stoned or something?" Jenn says. Her voice is carefully modulated, free of prejudice.

Gregory blows through his cheeks.

"No, not stoned, just very dimwitted." He extends an arm out in front of her, points impatiently for the water bottle. She passes him the plastic container, warm now, and he drains the remaining few inches in one go. He holds it out for Jenn to take back. Her hand stays resolutely on her lap, forcing him to slot the empty bottle in the side compartment of his door.

"What now then?" She sighs. "Can we turn back and go another way?"

"Jenn. Sóller is just *there*," he whines, pointing across the bay.

She hunches her shoulders and stares out of the window. Greg runs a finger down the side of her arm and overcompensates with a smile. He points once more to the honey-colored town resting in the bowl of the valley. "*Diez minutos*, once this prick gets his act together."

The van stutters forward, rolls back. Back and forth, back and forth—it goes on in this vein. Greg shuts down the engine, sticks his head out the window with his eyes shut to the sun.

"You might want to call the restaurant, Jenn. Tell them to push us back."

"I didn't book," she murmurs.

Still leaning out of the window, he grunts at the earthen cliff face.

"Guess we'll be eating in the square after all then."

"Come on, Greg! When have we ever, in all our time coming here, needed to make a lunch reservation? Even at the feted Residencia," and there's an edge to *feted*. "We walked straight in last year and bagged a prime spec."

He reaches out, finds her knee, and gently taps it. Taps out a little note of frustration. Like he always used to with Emma when she was younger, when he had to explain something about the world that she really ought to have known.

"Darling," he cocks his head, half turns to her. "When have we ever been here in high season?"

He's right of course. Until this year, they'd been habitual

crowd-dodgers. Early June or mid-September were favorites, but they'd been in deep mid-winter, too, and loved it. Emma's exams had put paid to that this year. July, the coach tours, this stifling, squalid heat—it was all brand-new to them. She sits low in her seat, feeling a touch martyred and badly regretting her decision to rise to him. The voice that comes from behind them takes them both by surprise.

"One of the rare privileges of a fee-paying school, I guess."

Greg rotates his whole upper body to face the unlikely antagonist. His top lip, curled up and pocked with beads of sweat, is trembling slightly.

"Privileges? How do you mean?" he says.

"License to take the kids out whenever you please." Nathan's voice is level, reasonable.

Jenn turns her head back to the cobalt sea, wishing with all her heart that she could stand on that stony ledge and plunge right off and in. She's with Nathan on the school thing, of course—but she can't let him know. It's Jenn who has stumped up the high season ransom—almost a thousand euros more expensive for their flights alone. It's Jenn who gave up chiding and debating the rights and wrongs with Greg, years ago. It's his little girl, after all. It's she who lost her mother, no matter what epithet Jenn bestows upon herself, whatever she does for Emma.

She can feel Greg bristling, hungry to take him on—but any kind of retort would seem churlish. Childish. There is nothing Greg can do but sit back, watch the van—and stew. The grating gear change, again; the engine revving madly, the jump forward, and the almost immediate listing back. Back and forth. The wheels spin wildly and the van jerks from side to side. For one moment it seems like the tires have got some purchase on the gritty surface, but then the engine cuts out and this time the van gathers pace, rolling back toward them.

Greg, still stewing, is slow on the uptake and Jenn reaches across and belts the horn with the balls of both fists. The van rolls and rolls. She can see it before he does and it is simple: If the van builds up enough momentum, it will push them over the cliff ledge.

Greg fires up the engine, spinning his head around wildly toward the back window to gauge their options. Bumper to bumper all the way back to the bend. "Fuck! Fuck!" He pumps the accelerator, slams into gear, moves forward a few feet and tries to reverse away from the edge of the cliff—but there's not much more than a foot or two of leeway before he realizes they're penned in. He gives it one last wild swing of the wheel and tries to move back, then he surrenders with a howl. He calls out her name and ducks down into the dashboard. And the moment is no longer than the space between the beat of her eyelids but it is enough.

Jenn hears the clap of a hunter's gun on the other side of the mountain. She opens her eyes. They are still there. In swerving to avoid them, the driver has plunged his van into a bumpy scrap of scrub, a foot or two below the bend on the other side of the road. Impatient drivers are already easing their way past, gesticulating at the driver, beeping their horns. Jenn turns around to find Nathan cradling Emma. He gives her a guilty look—*What else could I do?* Jenn is stung. Forlorn. Yet she feels the overbearing pulse of the moment. That was a line there, just then. That was it. From now on things will be different. Tonight she will set Nathan straight. Tomorrow he will tell Emma that the Nigel Godrich interview has been brought forward—and he will leave.

15.

She scopes the plaza, eyeing each of the terrace cafés in turn. There is not an empty table in sight. A procession of hopeful diners patrols the square, affecting nonchalance but ready to swoop the moment *La cuenta!* is called out. Greg and Emma sit on the church steps; Nathan is reading a plaque. Somehow the task of finding a table has fallen to Jenn, but it's too hot and the plaza is impossibly crowded. She takes shelter for a moment under an orange tree, ties her hair back, drawing out the ritual so the feeble breeze can air her armpits. She catches a whiff of herself—the metallic bite of panic gone stale. She finds her deodorant, sprays herself, and brings her arms back down to her sides. Right in front of her, two families begin squabbling over a table that's about to become available. She shuffles over to the throng of bodies that has grudgingly morphed into a queue outside one of the bigger cafés, changes her mind, and ambles over to the water fountain. Greg can see perfectly well what it's like down here. If he wants a table with a view so badly, he can fight for it himself. How can he even think that way? How can he walk away from a near-death experience and the first thing on his mind is lunch? And what was wrong with her suggestion anyway? A *bocadillo* in the café up by the tram station might not be nearly as quaint as the main square, but there's something gutsy and flavorsome about that café. It's real. Old men sit out back smoking all day and even their tobacco smells real, like her dad's used to.

She settles on the broad stone wall that surrounds the fountain. There is not much she can do to avoid the sear of the sun, but the spray soaks her dress, and she can feel the cold of the stone seeping through her thighs, and it feels good. She twists her upper body around and ladles water over her wrists. She can hear Greg's voice, authoritative yet strangely needy. She looks up and scans the square. She spots them on the other side of the plaza, by one of the expensive cafés with a bright red awning. Greg is making a beeline for a table, talking into his phone while pointing out Emma's crutches to the maître d' who gestures toward the patiently waiting queue. Greg holds his phone away for a moment and, seemingly, takes the restaurateur to task. He's shaking his head, pulling his embarrassed daughter close, as though to say: *Have a heart! Can't you see my daughter is crippled!* Nathan stands a couple of yards back, grimacing in apology to the others in the line. The flustered maître d' relents and shows them to a table that has barely been vacated by a couple of weathered old pensioners. Greg nods briefly, then pulls out a chair for Emma. She collapses into it, limp, dramatic. The old couple shuffles off, shaking their heads. Gregory goes back to his phone call, his hand alternating between his hair and the sweeping gesticulations with which he peppers the conversation. He ends the call, stares at his phone for a beat, then summons the waiter with a flourish of his big hand. He cranes and peruses the square. He looks directly at Jenn for a moment—but he does not see her. Only now does Nathan join them.

✼

Jenn slides off the cool stone balustrade and moves behind an orange tree to watch them. Nathan and Emma seem at ease in each other's company, as though they've been together for longer than four months. In their terms, by the law of young love, four months is forever. She thinks back to her own first love, how reaching the milestone of each month was celebrated as though it were a year. It felt like it would last forever. Water is being placed on the table. Nathan pours. First he sees to Emma, then he pours a glass for Greg. Greg makes no acknowledgment. He doesn't move. Then, as though snapping out of some reverie, he gets to his feet and pads away, holding up a finger to indicate he won't be long.

Nathan's eyes follow him a little furtively, Jenn thinks— and then she sees why. Nathan lowers his mouth to Emma's shoulder and drags his top lip down over her arm. He slips the slim strap of her dress down and licks along her collarbone. Emma slaps him playfully and looks over her shoulder for Greg. Nathan dips his hand in his water glass and takes out an ice cube. He runs it along her arm, his eyes never leaving hers. He puts the ice cube in his mouth and sucks it a while, then kisses it into her mouth.

Jenn turns away from them. She slumps back and lets the dry, slender trunk of the orange tree take her weight for a moment. She closes her eyes and it hits her again, hits her hard.

The breeze is rustling the leaves of the orange tree, and

farther away, the old wooden tram is trundling up from the little port. Only last week she and Greg were down on the harbor front, haggling for fresh-caught bass and squid. Jenn is not that woman. She is neither here nor there.

For a moment she can see herself standing in the doorway of a pub with the rain slamming down and the sound of laughter bellowing out from the smoky saloon. She can hear the low dirty rumble of buses on the other side of the estate. She is kneeling on the scratchy red carpet of her old living room by the three-bar fire; her dad is towel-drying her hair. He's giving her a lecture on the kind of low-life wretches she can't stay away from: the pretty boys with big lips and no soul; the boys in bands that hardly play; the poets who never write; the jobless dreamers. You're done with those kind of men now, Jennifer, her dad is telling her. She is twenty-nine. She lifts her eyes to meet his. She nods, and this time she means it. This time she listens.

※

She opens her eyes. Greg is back at the table; he's spotted her, or he thinks he has; he's slipping on his glasses and looking in her direction, pointing her out to Emma, and before Emma can confirm or beckon her over Jenn dips back behind the orange tree. She stands and waits and breathes, turns, and walks away from them.

She walks with her head down and her arms folded across her chest. She wants to get as far as possible from the square, into the warren of back streets that sit behind the town. She cuts across the broad steps of the church. Its massive wooden doors are open. Somber organ music hangs in the air. She could sit in a pew and let the stained-glass sunshine sieve her face. She could light a candle, say a prayer. She can sense him watching. Her footsteps echo across the church plateau. Shattered, she keeps on moving, moves on past.

The church is behind her now; she is lost in its shadow, out of sight. Free. She turns hard left up one of the narrow side streets and the chatter of the square ricochets down to nothing. It's cooler here in the alleyways, the pace is languid. Middle-aged couples stroll arm in arm, lingering at the tiny boutiques. Jenn traces a slow, sleepy zigzag in their wake, browsing from window to window. One of the shops seems only to sell chilies. They hang in bunches from the top of the window, every hue and texture, some waxy, shining, and ripe, others wizened. Next to it, a shop specializing in rugs: goat and rabbit skin, and one so thick it must be bearskin. Are there bears in the Tramuntana? There's an artisanal cheese shop; next to it, a jewelry shop specializing in ornate bracelets and chains. She stops and bends to examine the sea-grass baskets filled with bright, salvage-chic artifacts. And Jenn realizes, in a flash, that she is not free after all. Far from it. Even now she can feel a little hand on her wrist, tugging her, the girl with the gap between her teeth.

She was going to buy her something special, something symbolic to mark the years they'd been coming here, the times they'd had. She fingers a bracelet: beaten copper with studs of polished amber. She casts a sly glance through the open door. The pretty young sales assistant is chatting effusively with a couple. She slips the bracelet in her bag and walks quickly to the end of the street. Forks right, back into the blare of sunshine.

She turns off into a residential street. An arid gutter runs along its spine. The green wooden shutters are closed on the narrow town houses. Two old women sit on plastic chairs outside their front doors. They are ageless. Their eyes sparkle. They wear the same box hairstyles, the same formless frocks. They could be late forties; they could be well into their seventies. They chatter animatedly, fleshy arms flailing. They seem happy in their skin and age. A couple of scrawny cats weave in and out of their legs, tails held high. The women stop talking and gape as she passes. Their sun-beaten faces do not return her quick smile. They sit silent until Jenn is on up the road, and the chatter starts up once more.

She's in a narrow street now, no more than a dark and fetid passage. Rotten oranges and withered cloves of discarded garlic litter the cobbles. Her footsteps click and echo and, between her steps, there comes another, louder footfall. From nowhere, she feels the air-rush of someone coming up behind her. She clutches her handbag to her chest and tightens her elbows to her ribs. A hand grabs her by the shoulder and pulls her back. It's his—him. His hand drops down to link with hers. She grips him back, long enough to feel the awesome sensation rip through her, then flings her hand free and quickens her pace.

She tries to accelerate away from him but he's at her side again, and now he's in front of her. He spins around and walks backward, eyes never leaving hers. His pupils are black and huge; his skin, shiny with sweat. He tries to take her hand again. She puts both hands on his chest and pushes him away with force. He pauses for a while, as though making up his mind whether to leave her alone, and she strides away from him. She hears him, trotting to catch up with her and her heart gladdens with relief.

She is standing level with him now, her hands at her sides. She breathes across the adrenaline, striving for a calm authority.

"You're fucking her."

He doesn't say anything. And then: "You telling me or asking me?"

She is shocked and angry; angry that he doesn't deny it. She puts a hand on her stomach, looks away and down the street. A clutch of crones in the distance, dressed up. Going somewhere. She turns back to him.

"I'm asking you."

He drops his head, the smile dimple puckering his cheek. He shakes his head, still smiling, and looks her in the eye.

"Well let me ask you. Are you fucking the old man?"

The reaction is fast and deliberate. She slaps him once, across the face. The dimple is no more. Her hand hangs there on the recoil and he eyes it, incredulous. He places his hand on his cheek. Two old women are chuckling among themselves as they get closer. He moves into her. She doesn't resist. She can taste the salt through his T-shirt as she presses her face flat to it. She hooks a leg around his thigh so it's pressing between her legs, and she pushes down on it, so his dick digs into her. He scrapes up her hair from the nape of her neck, twists and holds it tight as he licks her throat.

"I need to see you," he says. "Properly."

❧

Over there. The café by the tram station. The unisex toilet down the spiral staircase. A waitress with heavily made-up eyes and a nose that is just a prolonged extension of her forehead passes them on her way up. It must be coming off their faces in waves. The waitress shoots them a look, her big loop earrings jangling as she shakes her head. Jenn makes fleeting eye contact, drops her head, and follows him into the cubicle. Nathan shuts the door behind them and slides the latch shut. The basin of the toilet stuffed with toilet paper; she thinks, No, no, not here—but then Nathan is turning her to face the big gilt wall mirror. He stands behind her, pulls her top, her bra down, licks and kisses her shoulders. She squirms. He stands back. Through the mirror, he forces her gaze down and over herself, lets her see just what this is. Their breath clouds the glass. He leans over her, his cock jutting into her hips, pushed back by his jeans. He licks a patch clear, looks her mirror image in the eye. She can't bear it any longer and she turns around and claws at his belt. He flips her back around. Places her hands on the mirror and pushes her face forward into the cool glass. One hand threads her tresses around his fingers. The other digs his cock out; tugs her knickers to one side. He sticks it in her cunt and pushes once, twice; then pulls it out and tries to put it into her arse. "Not that way," she mumbles and reaches down and feeds him back into her core. It is urgent and profound and it's over within seconds. She tries to hang on; she clenches her muscles to stop him sliding free; and when he does, some part of her comes away, too.

16.

From the doorway she watches him at work. Whatever he's writing, he means it: It's spewing from him in a fury. And yet, observing him now in the hard white glow of the desk lamp, his body has never looked so slack, so tired. The loose skin of his chest hangs down as he hunches over the pad. His skin looks lived-in; soon he will be like the crones in the backstreets. His pelt will hang from his body like old pajamas. Their history is inscribed all over those dimples and creases, his weathered hands. No extraordinary love story, theirs; defined not by drama or tragedy but by friendship. Faith. Mutual dependency. She watches him write and she is choked.

It whispers in her ear, the piece he read to her on their wedding day. It was an extract from a D. H. Lawrence poem.

> . . . *that is the crystal of peace, the slow hard jewel of trust,*
> *the sapphire of fidelity . . .*

She will always remember that, word for word—no matter what. She and Greg had hardly been together long enough for those words to have such resonance, yet the passage meant everything to her. It felt right.

She was a care assistant at Summerfields when they'd met. Greg cut a tragic, heroic figure. He'd lost his wife the year before, not long after she'd given birth to Emma. Greg and the little one used to come in every Saturday, without fail, to visit his mother-in-law. Not once did he miss a visit—not that she'd have noticed, old Irene. He'd recite poems to the patients in the dayroom, Keats or Shelley, she later found out. She thought they were his words, his poems. He'd incant the lines like he meant it, like those thoughts and words could only have emanated from him. The way his eyes would shine when he told her what he loved about poetry—the way you could own it. It became a part of you.

The old women in the home loved Greg. Her workmates loved him, too. He was handsome, after a fashion, Clark Gable with a beard. He wasn't really her type—too big, too manly. But he radiated some elemental *goodness* that she found attractive. He was nice. He was constant. And it worked— they were good together. Really good. Emma took to Jenn, and Jenn responded. She'd loved the sense of being needed. She loved snuggling up with Greg and resting her head on that broad chest once Emma was asleep.

He drops the pen on his pad and slumps back in his chair. He seems pleased with what he's written.

She clenches her fists and steps gently back out of the room and into the corridor, before he sees her. She gets out and down the steps, out of earshot. The force and fury of her sobbing sits her down among the rotting carcasses of the lemons, green welts pitting their dull, yellow-brown skin.

17.

"I don't trust him," she says as she forks hard left onto the switchback. It is early evening. It is one night and one day since the incident with the van on the cliff bend but, somehow, it feels much longer. It feels like Nathan has been here forever, and yet when she is not with him, when he is with Emma, time drags like tar. Farmers are tilling and raking their groves. A line of goats picks its way down the rocky incline; the toll of their maudlin bells. The light is soft and the landscape mellow.

"Who? Nathan?"

"Nathan."

Greg's eyes are on her for a moment, drilling the side of her face, then he turns away, gazing out to the slow-rippling sea beyond.

"Why? What's happened?" A snap of suspicion in his tone.

"Nothing's *happened*. Just a hunch, that's all."

She keeps her eyes trained on the road. A mountain rabbit flits across, pauses, and looks directly at them, then leaps to safety.

"I just think we need to be careful."

"Careful? Careful how?"

She rests her free hand on his leg and gives a reassuring squeeze.

"Look. It's nothing, right? Nothing at all—"

"It can't be *nothing*."

"It's just . . . I dunno. The way he looks at girls. You know?"

Greg is hunched forward in his seat now, his hands on his knees.

Her free hand is back on the wheel.

"Why? Has she said something?"

"Who, Emma? No!"

Greg sits back in his seat, drags his hands up his thighs, taps out a rhythm with his fingers. He's on the verge of saying something—and then he's stalling, thinking it through. She downshifts and slows to a crawl as she approaches the first hairpin bend.

"Because I looked it up, you know, this so-called blog of his."

"Yes?"

He doesn't answer right away. A lurch in her solar plexus. What has he seen? What has Nathan written? Something about *them*?

"And guess what?" He pauses for effect and drips irony into his expression. *"Site still under construction."*

Jenn relaxes. They turn into the dirt track up to the villa.

He releases his seat belt and shifts his whole body around to face her.

"Well?" he says.

"What?"

"Well what does that tell you?" Jenn lowers her chin, indicating for him to expand. "How likely is it that Godrich's people would approve an interview with a kid who doesn't even have a website?" Before she can respond, he adds: "So I asked Emma."

Jenn nods.

"I asked her if he'd be flying home early, for the *big* interview. She had no idea. Of course, she was quick to cover for him, but her first reaction was one of surprise. And the funny thing is, I knew it. I knew straightaway he was spinning you a yarn." He points a finger at her, vindicated.

Tell me Greg, *how* did you know? she wants to shout. She maintains a cool authority. "Possibly. Although couldn't it be that he didn't want to say anything until it was confirmed?"

And as though this were a game of chess, he considers it carefully before making his next move. He cranes his neck and rolls his gaze right up to the village where the young lovers are dining right now. "Do you not think it a little odd that he told you—and not Emma?" His eyes drill her again.

She gives an insouciant shrug of the shoulders but her neck is starting to burn. She badly regrets instigating this line of conversation. Her motive was simple: to throw a veil of doubt over Nathan's integrity, should he ever expose her. But she can see now there was no need. Greg had already cast him as the unreliable narrator—but now his sixth sense has fastened onto something else. She tries to kill it before it takes seed. She shrugs again and gives it her best poker face.

"Come on, Greg, isn't that obvious?"

"What?" He raises his eyebrows.

"He told me because he knew I'd tell you. I'm starting to find it just a little bit embarrassing—how desperate he is to

earn your respect. That's one thing we can be certain about—
the boy reveres you."

Greg dismisses this with a hiss. But Jenn knows her husband too well: There'll be a part of him that wants to believe,
a part of him that's flattered.

Jenn shuts down the engine. She turns to him, cups his
face with a hand.

"I knew I shouldn't have said anything. There's nothing
sinister about him, really. Just . . . let's be on standby, hey? Just
in case . . ."

She kisses him, hard on the mouth, and draws the conversation to an end.

They get out of the car and start unloading the shop-
ping from the boot. Jenn runs ahead to open the big wooden
doors. Greg lumps the carrier bags inside, four in each hand.
He takes the eggs out of their box and begins stacking them
in the fridge one by one, but with such force that Jenn fears
he'll break them.

"Tell me, Jenn," he mutters. "If there's something I need
to know, then please, tell me."

"Jesus! Are we still talking about that?"

"Well? Is there?"

"God. No. Nothing specifically . . . I mean, you know the
way men are. The silly little games they play. The lies they tell."

Gregory speaks slowly, deliberately into the fridge.

"He's not a man though, is he, Jennifer? He's a boy. And
he's your daughter's boyfriend."

If he'd have turned around he would have seen Jenn fighting back a furious flash of guilt. He finishes stacking the eggs
in their cup holes. It's all she can do to smooth her face out
and arrange her features in a way that roughly signals agree-

ment. She moves out of his eyesight, into the lounge. She hears him sigh deeply and then a bottle being uncorked. There's the glug-glug-glug as he fills his glass, full. He doesn't pour one for her.

"We having the pasta or the fish tonight?" he shouts through.

She waits until she's halfway up the stairs then shouts back, "Whichever. You decide. I'll be down in a mo. Just need my inhaler."

On the landing she pauses at that place. She shuts her eyes and tips her head back for a moment; it shoots through her again, almost as devastating as the first time. The moment she steps away it pulls at her, first from the inside and then from the outside, tugging her by the wrists, dragging her to the floor. She sits there with her back against the wall. He's out there with her, up at that little tapas bar at the end of the street. They are together on their tiny terrace, under the orange trees, hand in hand like lovers. And they are talking, animatedly. No—*he* is talking, and she is sitting there, all smiley and mute. He doesn't seek her opinion on anything, she's noticed that, it's enough that she's there, looking the part with her long legs and sun-blond hair, her honey brown skin. Even with her leg in plaster, she looked amazing going out this evening. Greg was almost tearful as he bid them fare-well. "There goes my little girl," he said. And now she's sitting there, his little girl too, sipping wine, looking into his eyes, agreeing with whatever he throws her way, and perhaps when they stumble back to the taxi hut later on, they'll slip off into one of the cobbled alleyways, and they'll kiss and his hand will slide up her thigh.

Jenn can't bear it.

The little gecko is back. It stays dead still, watching her from the other side of the wall. "What should I do?" she asks it. It watches her for a moment, scuttles up to the circular window, and slips out of sight. She's brought around by the sound of Greg calling her from the kitchen.

"When are we eating, then? Want me to start chopping peppers and stuff?"

Eating. Eat, eat—it's all he thinks about. Jenn doesn't respond, doesn't move. She hears him sighing again, impatient this time. He plods through and sinks into the sofa, a huge, solid plop as though he's simply fallen backward onto the seat. The television snaps into life. The roar of a crowd. Horns being blown. More wine being poured.

She just wants to be near him, just for a moment. She goes into his bedroom, sees the beaten-up jeans slung across the pine chair and touches their frayed hem lightly with her fingertips. She picks up his iPad, willing it to flicker to life, but it's locked. She wonders, briefly, why he didn't tell Emma about the Godrich interview. Perhaps it was exactly as she said: It didn't come off. He confided in her, though. She wishes she'd never mentioned it to Greg—but who else could she talk to about him? She lies on his bed; wraps her arms around his pillow. The smell of stale linen rises around her, and with it, him. She can taste the sweet-sour tang of his skin. She eases a hand down inside her knickers. Bites on the pillow. Rubs and rocks against herself until she comes. She lies there in a miserable, pitiful sweat. She can hear the crowd going wild downstairs, drums banging, hands clapping rhythmically. She can hear the excitement building in the commentator's voice.

Greg lets out a long wail that indicates whichever team he's rooting for came close to scoring.

In a few hours he'll be back, under the roof. Her heart buoys at the thought of it. Tomorrow she'll formulate a plan. She didn't get to see him at all today; Greg insisted that she come with them to the hospital. Nathan, without any hint of an apology or explanation, announced he was staying back to read his book. He'd caught her eye as he was saying it, but there was no way she could have wriggled out of this one; Greg asked her to drive. Although he'd never say so, he's shaken from yesterday's near-thing with the van. And anyway, that's where she *should* have been, at the hospital with their daughter. Not with him.

But tomorrow—tomorrow they will be together. Nathan has mentioned that his mother collects hand-painted tiles. Jenn can pretend she's driving him up to that little ceramics shop in Fornalutx. Emma won't want to trek up there. Not glamorous enough. They stopped off at the little village last year, cute and wanting to be arty, but there was nothing much of interest for the young. No way would Emma want to tag along; it'd just be Jenn and him. She'd drive him to that mountain bar on the road to Lluc. How he'd love it up there—the view would blow his mind! The glittering sea down below. The brutal ravine. They'd hold hands and gaze down beyond that terrifying drop, watch the waves smash the rocks. What was that Bjork song about the cliffs? No matter—there'd be no lecture from Greg about the scale and pace of the shifting coastline or any of the usual stuff he'd bore on about; no whining from Emma that her Coke is flat or the mosquitoes are targeting her and only her. It would be just the two of them. And she could see him now, his eyes misting over at the beauty of it all. He would see it and he'd feel it. He wouldn't need to say a thing, because she'd know.

Greg shouts up to her, trying to sound amenable, "Jenn? I'll put the pasta on, shall I?"

She's not fooled. She knows what he means. She swings a leg to the side of the bed.

"Two ticks."

Her toe hooks onto something as she stands, dragging it from under the bed. For a second the garment is suspended on the end of her big toe but, as she bends to retrieve it, it drops to the floor. Her chest crashes in on itself as she reaches to scoop the thing up. Her first thought is that the maid has not cleaned the villa properly after its previous occupants; no way does this item belong to her daughter. It is lacy and black and has little red bows around the hem. The gossamer across the crotch is virtually transparent and, all over it, there's the pearlescent smear of semen. She feels sick, sickened. Struck with grief.

"I'll do linguine tonight, then shall I? Jenn?"

She moves out of the bedroom and tries to find a voice.

"Lovely. Can you make a start on it?" She can hear the quaver; the keening as she shouts down to her husband. "I just need to jump in the shower."

He doesn't answer. Seconds later, the cupboards start to open and slam shut, the clang of pans.

She locks herself in the bathroom and strips and stands in front of the mirror and stares at herself with a hatred she hasn't felt since her acne years. The way her strap lines dig into her comfortable shoulders; her unruly pubic hair; her striated breasts, full enough but old, useless; that vein in her calf, starting to become raised and prominent; her stout arms, thick from all those years lifting old folk in and out of their baths, their beds. Dark crescents beneath her eyes; lines all around them, like knife cuts. The tips of her hair bleached dirty red by the pool's chlorine. An old woman, yes; she is old. Such a cruel trick of nature, she thinks, to age her body faster than it has aged her mind. She lifts her breasts with both hands and sucks in her stomach; she turns around and inspects her buttocks, bending slightly to tighten up the pits and dimples.

She steps back, smashed by the thought of Emma's skimpy black knickers, his residue. She feels sick all over again, and it's not just the one solitary betrayal. Jenn has bought Emma's underwear since she started secondary school. She understood the wiles and politicking of the changing room—or so she'd let herself think. She'd always opted for neutral colors—white, peach, navy blue—usually the kind of knowingly twee panties and matching cotton bras that speak of their owner's innocence, and their compliance in the postponement of womanhood. So it hurts enough to know that Emma, given the chance, had sneered at such virginal vestments. Even worse, though, is the crushing realization that, directly or indirectly, Nathan himself has selected those sluttish sex panties. Either he'd been there when she bought them or he'd told her what he liked. Did he really get a kick out of trussing his women up like hookers? And if so, what does he make of Jenn's choice of underwear? Her white cotton briefs and wireless brassieres? She turns back to face the mirror and cackles at her own stupidity. For fuck's sake, Jenn! A boy. A ripe and beautiful manboy. Who were you trying to fool?

She runs a bath. Digs out Greg's razor and slots a brand-new cartridge in. She smarts at how petty, how angry he would be if he knew she was using one of his precious blades. She submerges herself, and instead of trimming carefully around her bikini line, she takes the whole thing off. She doesn't bother to rinse the razor. Just puts it back in Greg's wash bag.

18.

At first, she thinks he is laughing. She has ferried out the pan of scallop linguine and gone back into the kitchen for the cheese. She knew Greg would approve: the hard, fresh, local mountain cheese he'd bought at the market, shaved with an apple peeler, just how he likes it. The light is dropping quickly and there is a smell of burning wood coming up from the beach. A wind kicking up. She hears the stifled hiccup of his laughter, or is it the catch of sobbing? Is he upstairs? It comes again, a smothered squeal. She looks out of the window and sees nothing, only the candle on the table he's laid. She's about to turn back to the pasta, and it's the faintest movement, a juddering rise and fall, that catches her eye. Greg is out there, slumped forward in his chair, his chin skittering off his chest as he sobs. She edges out of the patio door but stays by the steps, unsure what to do. Greg's shoulders lurch up and down, as he tries to stem his crying. He is gripping his wineglass; drops of Rioja splash over him with each new spasm. She goes to him.

"Greg..."

His crying is like a bird pecking at wet bark, relentless

yet strangely muffled. He lifts his face to meet hers for a brief moment, but shamed at her seeing him like this, he turns his head away, so he's looking out at the falling sun, big and rusty now, blazing on the edge of the world. He seems to compose himself, but then his shoulders start to tremble again, the anguish building the more he tries to hold it down. She takes a step toward him, but somehow she can't see it through. The sight of his big, solid frame crumpled, reduced to this, is alien to her. And along with the compassion, there's fear. Does he suspect? All that talk before—your daughter's boyfriend— does he *know*? She is winded all over again by the folly, the madness of this. She despises what she is, what she's doing here. She squats down next to him, takes his hand, and kisses it gently.

"Greg. Honey . . ."

She is looking up at him, but he won't meet her eyes. He can't look at her. He stares at the flickering candle, watches the flame dance back and forth on the tuft of yellow wick. He sips on his wine and places the glass on the table, rotating the neck of it between two fingers. The dark red liquid swirls around and around.

"Tell me what it is, baby," she asks, feebly, and puts her hand on his wrist. He looks at her hand for a long moment, like he's viewing it for the first time. He fingers her wedding ring. A needle of fear splits her. She knows, now, what is coming. However he frames it, however much she wants to purge, she will not confess. Deny, deny, deny.

It's coming. He draws up his chest, blows out through his cheeks. Her heart thumps wildly in her ears. She can feel her airways tightening up. In her head she tries to visualize her inhaler—her iron lung. He turns his body around to her. He can only look at her for so long before he's forced to turn away as if fearful of breaking down. He takes a sip of wine. Steels himself.

"I know what they mean now when they say your life flashes before you. There is no better way of describing it. It was there, right in front of me, all those memories that would make the final cut if..." He stifles a snuffle, pinches the bridge of his nose, and screws his eyes shut, then open again. "It was there and then, in a flash, gone."

"The van thing? Yesterday?"

He nods. "I thought we were..." He is still focusing on the candle. Its flame is beginning to lick flickering shadows across the table in the dimming light. He looks at her, suddenly. "See, I always told myself that if you really wanted a child of your own that bad, then you would have said. You would have pushed. But I know now that you wouldn't, would you? You didn't. Because you've never pushed me on anything. It's not in your nature. And it's too late and I'm so sorry."

He gets up and walks to the edge of the terrace, places both hands on the wooden railing. She follows and stands next to him. The sun has faded to a weak pink slit. In the twilight the lemon trees, their leaves absorbed by the dulling light, look like skeletal sentinels. She grips his wrists.

"You're in shock, Greg. How stupid of me! How fucking stupid..."

She can barely control the relief that is passing through her. He doesn't know at all. She holds his face in both hands, makes him look at her.

"How did I not pick up on that? The not being able to

drive the car, the way you've been since yesterday . . ." She can't disguise her glee. She'll forgive him anything. *Anything.* "It's fine, darling. All of it."

"Is it?"

She nods and tries to convey absolute certainty.

"I hope so, Jenn. I do so hope we'll be okay. More than you know . . ."

She smiles and kisses each hand. She moves away from the terrace and sits down at the table. The sun has slipped from view. The sky is darkening.

�֍

They joke about Benni and his impromptu appearances that always seem to coincide with Emma sunbathing by the pool; they talk about what they will do tomorrow. They do not mention the near-crash with the hippie van and they do not talk about each other. They finish the wine and each convinces the other that the cold linguine is the best meal of the holiday. It's delicious. They stand at the kitchen sink later on, washing and drying the dishes, mountain bats flitting in and out of the window. She casts a glance at her husband. He is miles away, absolutely lost in his thoughts. We'll be fine, she tells herself—and she reaches up and kisses the top of his arm to let him know.

She squats on the floor to get at the shelves behind the small gingham curtains. We'll be fine, she tells herself again, and she stacks the plates carefully, setting them down one-by-one, as though any sudden movement might shatter her conviction.

19.

She is seated at the kitchen table when she hears the rattle of the taxi's approach. The headlights come blinking through the lemon grove, the beams jolting up and down with each pothole. She blows out the candle. Its pear-shaped flame is frail and thin, burned right down to the wick. In its time, she has paced the kitchen floor in a fever of guilt, anger, recrimination.

She goes through to the lounge. Greg is sprawled across the couch, snoring, his glasses lopsided on his nose. Flickers from the TV screen reflect in their lenses. He is one big mass, taking up the entire sofa. She used to love the sense of constancy that his sheer size gave out. Now he seems unwieldy.

She places a hand on his shoulder and gently shakes him awake.

"They're back now, honey. Let's go to bed."

He whistles a stream of stale breath in her face, shifts position, grunts his annoyance at being disturbed. Jenn takes the throw from the end of the sofa and places it over him. Removes his glasses. She stoops to kiss his forehead, a wave of sadness rinsing over her. His phone drops onto the rug. The little red light is flashing. She picks it up, sees the four missed calls. It'll be the uni again, pestering him over the student-ships they're interviewing for. She wishes he'd be as assertive with work as he is dogmatic and insistent with herself and Emma. She places the phone next to the television so he'll see it when he wakes, then turns to take herself off to bed. The winking BlackBerry catches her eye, though, and she's overcome by a gnawing dread. What if those missed calls are from Emma? What if they've had an argument up there and drunk, or guilty, Nathan has confessed? There's a hot spray in her throat as she clicks the button with her thumb to bring up the call log, and then mild irritation. PROF. That's all. Thank God! Four missed calls from Professor Christopher Burns, one of Greg's oldest friends and a colleague. She hears the slam of the taxi doors and hurries up the stairs. Once Emma is in bed—once Jenn is certain she's asleep—she will go to Nathan and confront him. She will go to his room and have him tell her the whole sordid truth.

She is halfway along the landing when she's stopped dead in her tracks by a rapid series of beeps from below. She peers down to the terrace. A silhouette of two military-looking fig-ures staring up at the windows, and then a radio voice crackles. She would know that sound anywhere—Manchester, Roch-dale, Deià—it's the same all over the world. Trouble.

Two things go through her head as she hastens back down the stairs and sees the police car through the window: the incident with the hippie van yesterday, and the bracelet she stole. It is still in her bag, hanging behind the kitchen door. For one moment she thinks about dumping it in the bin but in the next realizes that in doing so, she'll be giving undue credence to her paranoia. Instead she places both hands on the door and breathes through her misgivings. Composed, she goes out to the terrace.

One of the male officers is fielding a call on the radio. His bulky, dark-skinned partner is sizing up the villa from the driveway. He has a hard, sly face that she takes against on sight. He pushes his shoulders back, stretches, and gives a world-weary crack of his knuckles, muttering something under his breath. She is standing there on the doorstep, no more than a few feet away; neither officer has yet acknowledged her presence. What *is* this? A combination of the cold night air and the lateness of the hour sobers Jenn to the reality that this is no trivial follow-up call. It's something serious—it has to be. She's about to go and rouse Greg when the guy with the sly face opens the back door of the car. A crutch pokes out first then Emma's face pops up above the roof. Her head hangs at a slant, and even from here, with only the dirty glow of the exterior lights to go by, Jenn can see that her eyes are squiffy. Their daughter is drunk, that's all, and the *policia local* have come to rub their noses in it.

She elects not to wake Greg, knowing how he'll react, and instead closes the heavy door behind her. Tiny stones and thorns poke her feet as she treads the drive barefooted toward them. Emma hobbles a little way to meet her. Jenn revises her opinion—she is not drunk at all. Her face is pink and peeling, puffy from crying.

"What's happened? Are you okay?"

She takes Emma's face between her fingers and looks right into her eyes. Emma focuses on her for one sharp moment before sliding off behind her. Her nostrils flare as though she's on the verge of tears again. Jenn turns to the *guardia*.

"What's going on here?"

The guy with the sly face looks at her and smirks. He delays answering, rakes his eye all over her as he lights a cigarette; he slows down the ritual, blows a long bar of smoke out across the pool.

"Nice place you got here."

He's regarding her lasciviously now; he's sinister. There's something about the sense of entitlement he radiates that makes her step closer to Emma and link a protective arm around her. She turns back to face the villa and gently tugs Emma with her.

"If that's everything, gentlemen . . ."

The cop is still grinning as though he knows Jenn's most intimate, recent, depraved secret. He blows another bar of smoke out and flicks the smoldering butt into the grove. His partner gets back in the car. Jenn's throat slackens a little.

"Next time, Momma, give her number for taxi, yes?"

He takes in the villa one last time then slumps down into the car and slams the door. They reverse at crazy speed back down the track, spinning out onto the narrow beach road and tearing back up the steep sidewinder to Deià. Their taillights watch her from on high.

Jenn goes to help Emma indoors, but she shrugs her off angrily. She shuffles through the side gate toward the swimming pool, lowers herself onto the steps, and just sits there in silence, staring out across the bay.

"Emma?"

No answer.

"Em."

Emma turns her shoulders to indicate that she'd like to

be left alone, her chin jutting out self-righteously, just like her father does. Jenn knows she should leave her be—but she has to know what has taken place up in the village tonight. She dips inside, returns with a bottle of wine and two glasses. She pours out a glass, hands it to Emma.

"Come on. What happened, darling?" she says. Her stomach turns as she awaits the response. She wants to ask, Where is Nathan? Stop your sniveling and tell me what has happened to Nathan. But no sooner does the question declare itself than Jenn recognizes the depravity of it all. This must stop now—and she must end it, as soon as he is back.

Emma reaches into her canvas satchel and takes out a packet of cigarettes. She slides her eyes across at Jenn—not to seek her approval but to slap down any hint of resistance. Jenn doesn't flinch. She squeezes out a smile that says, Of course I know your secrets. I know you smoke. I know about your spunk-sprayed underwear. She leans across and takes a cigarette for herself. And now it's Emma's turn to look surprised. Yes, Emma—I am old. I am finished. But I have secrets, too. Jenn studies her in the flame, her tiny nose, dusted with freckles, and she is smitten with guilt. Not so very long ago she used to count each and every one of those freckles; she'd pretend that two had gone missing, they were hiding up her nose or in her ear, and Emma would fall back giggling and say, "Again, Mummy! Count again!" They scrutinize each other through drifts of smoke. Emma exhales, holds up her cigarette, and says, "Don't tell Dad about the police bringing me back."

She draws deep on the cigarette, as though to show Jenn just how long she's been doing this, how little Jenn really knows about her. She holds the third drag in, lets it out slowly, in waves. Jenn tops up Emma's wine. She's barely sipped at her own. She changes tack, changes her tone. She speaks to her as she might speak to a friend.

"Did you two fight?" Jenn asks. Emma shrugs. "Do you want to talk about it?"

Emma drops her head. "Not especially." She draws on her cigarette, tilting her head back as she exhales into the night vault. She stays like that, staring up into the sky. The stars are blunted, the moon covered by cloud.

"Okay." Jenn gets up, smiles. She's cold, but she can hear the added shiver in her voice. This is her and Emma now. No joy. No love. Fear is all there is. "You enjoy your smoke. I'll come and get you in a bit. Help you up to bed."

Jenn turns to go. Emma brings her gaze down slowly from the stars.

"We argued about you, actually. Seeing as you ask."

Jenn tries to swallow her own bile.

"*Me?* Why would you argue about me?" Her delivery is so swift, so seamless in its execution that even if her daughter did suspect it of her, she might think twice now. Emma's nostrils are flaring and shutting.

"He said you deserved better."

"Nathan did?"

"Yes. Nathan did. He said you deserved better than Dad. He said Dad didn't know how to handle a woman like you. That if you were his wife, he'd know how to handle—you."

"Why would he say that?"

"I don't know." She watches Jenn. "Why would he?"

Jenn can't meet her eyes. She can hear the falsity in her tone. "I hope you put him right!"

Emma holds her gaze for a moment longer, then she digs into her canvas bag, pulls out her wallet. Jenn's heart begins to bang, hard. She eyes the wallet, expecting Emma to produce some irrefutable piece of evidence; whatever Nathan has been writing, she's about to be confronted with it. Her face must nakedly display the shock that seizes her when Emma slaps a credit card on the table. It's Jenn's AmEx. She picks the card up, squints at the name, just to make sure.

"Where did you—"

"Dad."

"Your father gave this to you?"

"Loaned. But only because his card hasn't been working. He said he'd reimburse you as soon as we get back."

Jenn is fighting to get on top of her anger at the sheer effrontery of it.

"Well it would have been nice for your father to check with me that mine's working okay. Did it?" Emma tries to tough it out with a shrug, but her lip is beginning to tremble. "Why did you need, it anyway? There's cash enough in the house for a meal out."

"Dad booked us into Jaume. He wanted us to have something special to look back on."

And this last bit has her boiling over again. She squats so she's level with Emma's face. When Emma tries to look away, Jenn takes her chin between two fingers and gently, firmly turns her head back toward her.

"He had no right."

"I know! Okay? I fucking well know you wouldn't have let us!"

She jabs at her with spite-sparkled eyes. Jenn can only whisper her response.

"You're damned right I wouldn't." She has to walk away to the far end of the grove just to let go of her anger. She takes her time coming back. "Do you not see how . . . *wrong* that is? You have to *earn* privileges like that, Emma. Jaume! And how *were* you going to pay us back?"

She gives a lopsided grin. "Well I could try for that *weekend* job you're always on my back about." She screws up her face, broadens her vowels, and starts to imitate Jenn. "Hey, maybe then I would have earned the privilege, right?"

It's been coming for some time, this. Jenn can feel it surging up, thrumming through her in waves. She knows she will, on this point, regret anything she says but can't keep a lid on it. She tries to keep her voice calm, clipped.

"Do you know, darling, I probably wouldn't have minded if you'd have asked me." Emma rolls her eyes, and Jenn flips. As she starts talking, an inner motor takes over, speeds her up until there's no Jenn left, there's just her voice, talking. "Emma—if you *were* that person who *had* a job, who *took* responsibility for your own actions, then you *would* have run it by me. But you're not that person, are you? And judging by that little stunt you pulled tonight, you show no signs of growing into her. And for the record, if you want to play grown-ups with your boyfriend in some nice fancy restaurant then you need to start acting like a grown-up. You need to get out of this mind-set that you just *get* things by pouting. By intimidation . . ." She was getting out of breath, but she couldn't stop. "Start *working* for the things you want so bloody badly! And before you start pulling your faces and rolling your eyes, the answer's yes. You need to start doing what I did at your age, like I'm doing now—six, seven days a week plus overtime to pay for your fucking education! To pay for those privileges you take for granted."

Emma drags herself to her feet, gets one crutch under her armpit.

"Nice speech, *Jenn*. You must have been working on that for weeks—"

"Years." She's gone too far. She can't stop swinging at her. Emma smiles. She is calm. There's emotion, but she's measured.

"I'm sorry it's all such a big sacrifice for you, Jennifer. You're so damn martyred aren't you? Having to provide for me, having to pay my school fees. It must be some burden, all that..." She makes a big thing of stooping for the other crutch. Shuffles a step closer to Jenn. "I know I've never, ever heard any of my friends' mums harping on like you do. Never heard one of them moaning about all the sacrifices they make, all the hours they put into giving their kids this great, fantastic life."

Jenn is possessed, now. She pokes her finger into Emma's chest. "Your friends' mothers don't even work! They wouldn't know sacrifice if it slapped them in the face!"

Emma sneers at her, looks her up and down. "That's because it's not sacrifice to them. They do it because they want to. And that's the thing, Jenn, you do it because you have to—and don't you let me know it."

She drags herself down the path, hesitating at the little broken gate. She rests a crutch against the gatepost and leans down to pull it open. Its bottom sticks in the grit. Mortally wounded, Jenn comes up behind her. The rasp of her breath is loud as she pulls Emma back by the shoulder.

"Maybe that's because you're not my kid!"

There's the flicker of something in Emma's eye. Victory. She smiles and hobbles off. Jenn just stands there, numb. She is shivering. Silence, except for the wheeze of her lungs. She heads back inside the house. Slips on her sandals and scoops up her handbag, digging out her inhaler as she gets in the car and fires up the engine.

20.

She crawls along the narrow road to the village, eyes scanning right and left. The dark is nearly solid and with no moon to light the way, she sits with her face right up to the wheel. She snaps on the full beams; at any moment she expects to see his figure loom into view. She is desperate to see him; she doesn't see him. She passes the police car, pulled in at the bus stop by La Residencia. The inside lights are on and their heads are bent over something. Porn, no doubt. She slows to twenty. She is a good few units of alcohol over the limit; she'll give them no excuse.

The restaurants are all closed but she can see Bar Luna's tree lights twinkling in the night breeze. She slows down as she passes. Thinks she spots him leaning against the terrace balcony, his arms stretched out along the banister. She winds her window down but does not stop; laughter and the buzz of chatter. She is not ready for him yet. She carries on down the village road, closes her eyes as she passes Jaume. The road darkens as she passes the font and starts her climb back up and out. Through the blackness she can just about trace the outline of the olive groves below, like a giant staircase racing to the sea. The road is wide and straight for a while and she presses her foot down hard. The surge of speed soothes her, and she thinks back to Emma.

Words that needed to be said. Words that cannot be unsaid. It's been hovering there, hovering between them for months. She could never bring herself to analyze the whys and hows, but she's felt it coming. Emma's questions, Emma's fury. She knew, yet she had no inkling of the extent, the depth of feeling—and this time she can't just brush it off as a teenage outburst. This felt rehearsed, as though it was coming from someone much more mature. Jenn had felt like a foolish girl. Emma sounded like a woman.

She forks right after the garage. For a few miles she is moving inland through the mountains and the darkness closes in on her like fog, but then the road bends back on itself and the sea slides into view. Shiny, a sheet of dark metal, lit up by a slither of a moon, clouds blown fast across the sky. Maybe he was right after all. When they met, when they became official, it was Greg's wish that they kept things simple with Emma until she was older. Yes of course he'd tell her about her birth mum in good time, but for now there was no point confusing her. Jenn fought him on this: When she moved in with him she dug out the crates of photographs and memories that Greg had consigned to the attic, found a picture of Emma's mother, and installed it on the mantel. In Emma's bedroom, she hung a picture of her as a newborn in her mother's arms, taken only hours before her mother died. Gregory took down the pictures. He was furious. "Let her call you Mum. We'll tell her when she's ready." She didn't have it in her to hurt him, to say, "But *I'm* not ready."

When Emma first said it, it made her feel trapped. Mama. For the first time in her life she was made rudely aware that she was accountable to someone other than herself—and it scared her. She couldn't flee if things didn't work out between her and Greg, and she knew that if she went through with this whole thing, if she walked down that aisle with him, she'd be pledging her vows to two people, not one.

The road twists through dense pine forests. The moon slips out of sight. A mountain hare flits across the road and she swerves to miss it. A steep incline, flashes of streetlights through the trees. She lets her foot off the accelerator, coasts for a while. She recognizes some of the places on the road signs. Banyalbufar. There's a bar there they visited one winter that Nathan would love—shabby, mainly locals, cheap, and real. She wishes he were here right now, by her side, his hand on her lap. She wishes they had Deià to themselves. She wonders if she could bring him back here, just the two of them. Greg was always on at her to extend her horizons. Perhaps she will. Perhaps she'll do just that.

The road dips down and away from the mountains. The flat black disk of sea below as she coasts around a bend and down toward the village. She'll dip into the bar for one large brandy, then it's back home again to face up to things. To find him and sort this whole mess out.

She is woebegone. The bar is no longer there. In its place is two-thirds of a villa. She stifles a resentful laugh, parks, shuts off the engine, goes over to inspect. She can picture the place in her mind's eye. Paco's. Tatty. Lively. Full of smoke and laughter. Yes, Nathan would have loved it. She crosses back to the car. A solitary old man gives her a look as he passes by. She starts to get back in the car, steadies herself on the door.

"Excuse me?"

He stops. She tries a smile. Nothing from him.

"*Parle inglese?*"

A shrug. Maybe. Depends.

"The bar?"

His face splits and creases into a sad smile. "Ah, Paco's place? You remember this?"

Jenn nods.

"Yes. I remember Paco's. I remember it good." He shrugs again. "Gone. No people. Everything change."

He gives her the slightest bow—a tiny nod of the head and shoulders—and he's on his way. Jenn gets in the car, drives through the little town as far as the cliffside car park, turns around. Sets off back toward Deià.

The night sky is perfectly black. The wind rocks the car. She drives on, thinking nothing—but then Deià curves into view below, the church lit up like a beacon in the starless night, and it all starts to seep through her again. The whole thing feels like a landslide; the more she digs, the more it submerges her. She could drive straight back to their villa and go straight to bed, and in the morning, the storm will have worn itself out. Emma will be contrite, sullen, and a little embarrassed, but she'll want to make things up with her. Greg will be Greg. All will be well again.

She passes Sa Pedrissa on her left, Deià now a minute or two away, and the bar where she thought she saw Nathan, and she finds herself overcome by the deepest conviction that no, all will not be well again. Things won't be the same from now on. Words were said, opinions expressed that cannot be taken back.

"Everything change."

There's no going back now. Emma said things. Jenn said worse, and it will take her years to earn back Emma's favors, not that she won't try her damnedest but those mother-daughter privileges were never hers to earn in the first place.

21.

She steels herself. Heads up Bar Luna's narrow steps.
Nathan has moved deeper into the crowd. He's leaning against
one of the chunky wooden stanchions, smoking, nonchalant.
She can just about make out a slice of his shoulder and brown
forearm as he lifts the cigarette to his lips. The terrace is
filled with locals of all ages: the teenage progeny of expats;
arty octogenarians; the flirty young sales assistant who sold
her the frock the other day; and lots of svelte young women
with beaded hair, all vying for the attention of a good-looking
white guy with fat, fuzzy dreadlocks. Eyes shut, hands behind
his back, he sways minimally to the dirty dub beat, thoroughly
aware of his admirers looking on.

A man swaggers toward her, moving his shoulders in time
to the music. He's some kind of local "face," from the way he
propels himself from exchange to exchange, kissing cheeks
and shaking hands as he moves through the crowd. At a distance he's lithe and impressive, like a European rock star. But
the terrace floodlights do him no favors as he gets closer. His
skin is leathery; all she can see is a set of brilliant white teeth

coming at her, his weather-bleached hair. He stands a yard away and bows.

"Oh welcome, mysterious lady."

He means no harm, yet he infuriates her. She ducks her head and pushes right past him.

Jenn is by no means the oldest in here and yet she feels, suddenly, horribly aware of her age. She hates the word—has mocked Emma, gently, for her overuse of it—but Jennifer from Rochdale is not *cool*. She feels it with every clumsy step as she goes to seek out her beau.

He's in the corner holding court with a gang of young Londoners. Their laughter is loud and self-possessed—and it grates on her. There was a time, not that long ago, when the only English accents they heard in Deià were their own. The thought saddens her as she stands off and watches him, a manly boy, laughing hard at some caustic remark. She composes herself. She's not nostalgic, just sad.

Nathan still hasn't seen her. She's right behind him now, within touching distance, and she can barely contain her nervous excitement. The smell of weed is so strong in this corner of the terrace that she feels light-headed just inhaling. She reaches forward, takes the cigarette from his fingers, and places it between her lips. He jerks around angrily, and his face flits from shock to fear to guilt with each panicky blink of his eyes. And then she sees why.

She's on the other side of the column, but she's definitely with him. Her. The hippie girl from the beach cave, the one he flirted with at the market stall. Her slender fingers are drumming out a note of intimacy on the nape of his neck. Jenn's eyes are transfixed by her cheap rings, two or three on each finger, rising and falling as she strums. Can't think, can't breathe. Nathan extricates himself and tries to look happy and surprised. His face radiates terror.

"Jenn! What are you . . ."

She smiles icily. Says nothing. She turns her eyes on the girl. Nathan steps back as though noticing her properly for the first time. "Have you met Monica? Here, let me get you a drink."

She feels she may collapse if she doesn't go now. She spins and pushes her way back through the crowded terrace. The teeth man tries to block her path and insinuate her into his dance. She drops her shoulder and barges him out of the way.

"Prick!" she spits out.

She clatters along the empty road with her arms folded, her unsteady footsteps ringing out. Her throat starts to tighten. She slows down, dips in her bag for her inhaler. Blasts. She knows he's behind her. She can neither see him nor hear him, but she senses him keenly. She increases her pace. She's right at the car, zapping the lock, when she hears the slap of his Converses sprinting to catch her. He stands flat against the driver's door, his arms out to either side. She points the key at his face.

"Move!"

She puts both hands on his upper arm and tries to shove him out of the way. He laughs, but he's worried.

"Jenn, just let us explain, yeah?"

"No need."

She jabs the key at him again. "Tomorrow I am booking your flight home. When you get home, you break it up as gently and as nicely as you can with my daughter. You do not contact any of us. If you do . . . if you dare breathe a word to anyone, I swear—"

"Your daughter?" he says with a sneer.

A sharp intake of breath. A current running through her, mad, dangerous. She tries to contain it but, as she looks up, his face is all scorn. It's hateful. She snaps her arm at him. The key scrapes his face; it makes the sound of a zip being pulled down fast. His hand shoots up to the spot. A tear of blood rolls down between his fingers.

"I'm sorry . . ."

She puts her hand on top of his and tries to convey it with her eyes; she can't bear that she's hurt him.

"Why are you here?" His eyes are dancing with indignation. Jenn says nothing. He's got her. He moves in for the kill. "Emma?" He smirks and shakes his head. "Want to know why Emma stormed off?"

"I can hazard a guess." She flicks her eyes over her shoulder, toward Jaume. "Actually, no. She's already told me what happened—"

"Has she? I bet she didn't tell you that we made up, did she? That she was begging me to take her back to the villa and fuck her on the sun lounger, right under your window." Jenn lurches back like a woman slapped. There's something in his eyes, the injured tone of voice, that tells her he's not lying. "Tonight. It was going to be the night. After our fancy meal in the restaurant."

She takes off her cotton cardigan, folds it over, and presses it against his cheek. She looks him directly in the eye. "So all those other times she's been in your bed, does that count for nothing?"

A brief flash of something in his eyes, but he recovers quickly. "My bed? Oh yeah, right! And how does that work then when she's on crutches?"

She drops her hand from his cheek so she can see his reaction. "I found her knickers in your bed."

His eyes dart all over her face. He licks his lips and goes on the front foot. "Oh yeah, really? And what else did you find while you were snooping around my room?"

She reaches behind him for the door handle. "I wasn't snooping—"

"Sounds like it to me. I reckon you got a kick."

She goes to strike him again. Drops her head, ashamed. Nathan moves closer. He lowers his voice.

"Look. I don't know what you found or how they got there. Maybe from another family, hey?"

"No." She gives him a weary smile. "They were Emma's."

"Sounds like you *want* them to be Emma's. You want an excuse."

"Your semen had barely dried on them, Nathan."

And this time he's shocked. Again the resigned, downward smile. She touches him lightly. "I'm sorry I hurt your face. But please can you move now, I want to get in the car and go home."

He holds her look for a beat, then steps away from the door. She gets in. He flips around and grips the door so she can't pull it shut.

"Not that it's any of your business, seeing as you've already reached your verdict on me . . ." A glisten of tears in the corner of his eyes. "But Emma was not and has never been in my bed. Not here, not back at home."

Jenn just sits there. She doesn't believe a word of it. She is desperate to believe it. He swallows, pauses, and forces her to look him in the eye.

"We made do. She shoved them under, after—" He breaks off. "Just use your imagination, yeah?"

She mulls this over. Is it any better, any easier that he hadn't actually penetrated her? Jenn had been right the first time. Emma and Nathan had done everything but.

"So why hold out, Nathan? If Emma wanted it *so* badly . . . why not give her what she wanted?"

He looks at Jenn, wide-eyed. "Er . . . because she's fifteen?" He phrases it as a question, just to make her sound stupid.

"I see." She points back at the bar. "And what about her? Is she of age? Or yet more forbidden fruit?"

Nathan shakes his head, slowly. "Can you stop this, Jenn."

"Believe me—I wish I could."

"I'm not like that."

"Looked very much to me as though you're very much like that—the way she was pawing you, hands all over you."

"Monica? Seriously?" He starts to chuckle as he digs into his pocket. "Oh my God, Jenn." He opens his palm to reveal a small plastic bag, half filled with skunk weed. "This is what Monica is to me." And the look he gives her is so hurt and childlike that she wants to hold him. "And that's what I am to her. A punter. A sale."

He starts to walk away from the car, stops, and turns back. He points through the door, right into Jenn's face. If she didn't believe him before, she believes him now.

"You have no right," he says softly. "*He* gets to go to bed with you and wake up with you." His lip is trembling. "He sees every part of you. You're his. Do you have any idea how that feels for me? Lying awake, listening? Imagining what you're doing..." He starts walking backward up the road. "Leave my passport and my bag on the terrace. I'll be gone by the time you wake up. You won't see me or hear from me again."

Through the rearview mirror she watches him walking back up the road, clutching his cheek. He walks right past Bar Luna, crosses over at the car park, and dips down toward the stream. She can feel herself falling as she starts up the car.

22.

It is past midnight when he returns. The moon has long since been consumed by the night and Jenn is huddled up on the steps, swaddled in a throw. The wind has an edge to it; it pulls her lungs tight. Every so often the gust drops to nothing, and through silence she hears Greg's snoring up above.

Nathan hasn't seen her. She slips down the steps and weaves in and out of the shrubs so she meets him from the side. The grass pokes through her sandals, rough and bone-dry from the wind. She takes him by surprise; his reflexes are sluggish and she wonders if he's stoned. Even in the dark she can see that his hair is flayed from the wind; she can smell the salt on his skin. Has he been sitting on the beach all this time? Was he alone? She dare not think it. She doesn't say a word. She takes him by the wrist, around the side of the house, leads him across the rocky soil to the farthest corner of the grove. A tiny patch of flat ground is lit up by the pool lights on the other side of the villa. She lays her throw down, gestures for him to sit.

She straddles him and kisses him, hard. He doesn't resist. His dick is already pushing up through his jeans. She pops the buttons on his fly. She can see the pool light bouncing off his watch as he helps her spring himself free.

She stands, and with her back to the villa she peels off her clothes, everything. Her tits tighten. She spits on her hand, rubs between her legs, and very slowly lowers herself onto him. Their faces are level, eyes wide open. He thinks it's a mistake; he reaches around for his dick, pulls it out, and guides it into her cunt. She pushes him out again, eyes never leaving his. She holds him down with one hand and maneuvers her thighs up and down until he's in properly. She grips tight to his biceps to steady herself against the tearing and stabbing.

"This is yours," she says. "Just you."

He nods; he seems to understand. His eyes don't blink, just stay pinned to hers, rapt. His thumb finds her, just to make sure, and then his pupils slip away, off into some space up there beyond the mountains and the fast-moving clouds.

❧

She skins up: It's been a long time, yet even in the rising wind the ritual is familiar to her. They lie back; scattered around her head are dozens of lemons, gone to seed. She can hear the crash of the ocean, the lowing of the wind beginning to whip. Her breathing is shallow as she sucks on the joint, holds it down. Somewhere on the terrace, a deck chair is being blown around. A door is slamming; the pool's lights flicker out.

23.

A light is being snapped on, a shutter is banging open, banging shut. The wind is keening through the house. Gregory is pacing the room, cursing. Jenn lies very still, wincing from the ceiling light as she tries to piece it together. She has a flashback to knocking the bedside lamp over as she fumbled her way into bed, Gregory scolding her. It feels like it was only moments ago.

Greg is talking to someone, but it is not her. She lifts her head from the pillow and sees Nathan standing in the doorway, clad in just his briefs. They both turn to her as she sits up in bed.

"Jenn," Greg says to her. "We have a . . . an issue."

Her guts twist. He knows—he has found out. She has never seen Greg look so afraid—so serious. He moves to the foot of the bed. He is wearing jeans and a coat. He sits down next to her, takes her hand. This is it.

"It's Emma. She's missing."

A gust slams one of the shutters hard against the wall. It concertinas open, then doubles over on itself, the wood splitting at the hinges. She can hear the waves slamming the bay, but it is nothing compared to the gale of queer relief that slams through her. Greg strides over and hooks the shutter to the wall. She reaches for her inhalers—Gregory has arranged them on her bedside table: the blue reliever closest to her pillow, and next to it, her pink preventer. She holds the cool spray deep in her lungs, stringing out the ritual as she scopes Nathan's face for clues. He looks straight at her but his eyes tell her nothing.

"Missing. How do you mean, missing?"

Greg stands at the window, chewing the tips of his knuckles as he watches the storm. The tops of pine trees are flailing against the blackness, like people fleeing disaster.

"She's not in her room, not in the garden. I've been up to the village. Her bed hasn't been slept in."

Jenn's default response at such times would typically be one of annoyance, directed at Greg more than at Emma. It was his overprotective, overly dramatic response to every little strop that, she felt, urged Emma on toward ever more elaborate revenge ruses. It was a game to her, a drawn-out but perfectly judged play. She would always go walkabout after a spat, no matter how trivial—she'd have to draw blood. And on each of those occasions, she would stay out just long enough for even Jenn to begin to fear the worst so that, when she *did* finally present herself at the front door, eyes sullen and challenging, the agony of her parents and their ire at the ploy was submerged by the joy of having her back again.

But last night wasn't like that. Last night had been no mere spat—no play. She had told Emma, in so many words, that she was nobody's daughter. Maybe this time Greg's instincts are right: Perhaps their daughter has gone. And the more Jenn dwells on it, the harder it is to chase the feeling. She can feel the dread gathering in the bellows of her stomach, the way she feels a storm in her chest. Something has happened, and she knows she is to blame. She said those things to Emma and now she's out there. Greg has no idea.

He comes over, squeezes her hand, tries to be reassuring—but his face is pinched and gray with fear. He turns to Nathan.

"I need you to talk me through it all again. Everything. From when you went for dinner in the village."

"Yeah, just like I told it." He lowers and raises his eyelids wearily. "Came back around eleven. Went straight to bed."

"And there was no . . . no argument? No misunderstanding or anything like that?"

"*No.*"

Jenn feels it rise in her throat. How can he look Greg in the eye and just plain *lie* like that? She holds the anger down, forces Nathan to catch her eye. He holds her gaze with a steady, challenging look. "What?" he is asking her, "What do you want me to say?"

Greg isn't buying it. He's weighing him up—the way he might look at a student who claims his laptop's been stolen the night before a deadline. Part of him wants to give the boy a chance, yet all his human experience persuades him otherwise. Nathan shifts his gaze to Greg, stares right at him with clear, unmoving eyes. With nothing to rely on but his instincts, Greg turns his attention to Jenn. For a moment he just stands there looking at her, as though he sees—he *knows*—everything. She concentrates on shaking her inhaler, theatrically blasting the gas down.

"Did . . . did you go out last night? In the car?" His tone isn't accusatory but pleading. He's trawling for clues, not a culprit. She is desperate to tell him—everything. She can't bring herself to say a word. They stare at each other. "I thought I heard the car."

If she is to tell him, it must be now. She finds herself focusing on a coarse spiral of pure white hair poking out from his nose. She despises him for it, for not knowing it's there.

"I went out for, you know," she slides a brief glance in Nathan's direction, lowers her voice, "women's necessities." She gets out of bed; realizes she is still in last night's dress, crumpled and grass-stained. There isn't so much as a questioning flicker from Greg. There's a head rush and she grips the bedside table to steady herself. She wafts her free hand in front of her face to intimate that her inhalers have made her light-headed. "I stopped off for a sandwich on the way back." And she could end the charade here. Greg has drifted away. His mind is already elsewhere, dredging for another line of inquiry, but as though she's working out the story as much for her own benefit as his, she carries on. "You remember that little place between Valldemossa and Banyalbufar? Paco's?"

"Paco's." He smiles, momentarily released from the ordeal. She nods, as though tuning into his nostalgia—they'd eaten there the winter they came. They'd driven straight from the airport in search of food; it was the only bar open and the kitchen had shut down for the evening. They were serving only *bocadillos*, but their twinkling host, Paco, was insistent that his English guests would have hot fare. He heated up *estofado de Tramuntana*—mountain stew, made from kid and rabbit— and made hand-cut fries for Emma. Greg talked about that meal for months. There is a picture on his desk of six-year-old Emma sitting on the bar.

He snaps back to the here and now. "Was she in her room when you came to bed?"

"I don't think so. I didn't think to check."

"You must have noticed if her light was on."

"I'm sorry, I . . ." She's floundering, and now Nathan is trying to catch her eye. See? You are no different than me.

Greg rubs his face, slumps on the bed. Nathan is still hovering in the door. They both look at him.

"I'll go try to phone her again," Nathan says.

Greg discharges him with a nod. They hear his room door shut and Greg leans into her and says, "He's lying about something."

"Oh, I don't know, Greg. Let's not jump to any conclusions, hey?"

"Something's not right. You said it yourself yesterday— you don't trust him." She sidles toward the bathroom, hesitates until she's certain she's dismissed. Greg is still hunched over, his hands clasped between his legs. "That fucking kid knows something, I'm sure of it. What else could possibly explain his indifference?"

His expression wanes from a livid self-righteousness to resigned, humble sadness. Jenn wants to go to him, to hold her husband, but she can smell herself: the sex sweat, the residue of skunk on her fingertips. And thinking back to him, to them, only hours ago, another fire is lit. Her daughter is missing; she fears for her. Yet she has to know who raised the alarm. Did Nathan go to her room to make up with her? Did he go there for sex and find her bed empty? She knows they are fucking—she knows it. But why does he still go to Emma? What does Emma give him that she does not?

She lets the doorframe take her weight and strains for a casual timbre.

"Was it you or Nathan who noticed she wasn't in her

room?" He shrugs as though the question is as trivial as it is self-evident. "Greg?"

"The big door downstairs . . . It was banging. It woke me up, so I went to have a look. It was wide open. I thought we might have been robbed at first, but everything seemed fine. On my way back up to bed I noticed Emma's lamp was on." Jenn blanches. He *does* know! Why ask her if she'd noticed whether Emma's light was on? Greg drones on, his voice utterly flat, defeated. "I stuck my head around the door expecting to find her reading . . ." He forces a rueful smile. "I was going to tell her to get her beauty sleep, you know . . . but she wasn't there and I assumed . . . I thought the worst. I went straight to *his* room expecting to find . . ." She nods, giddy with relief. He lowers his mouth to her ear. "I found this on her bed." He gets up, goes to his bedside drawer, takes out a book. *The Social Contract.* Jenn doesn't get it, she nods for him to elucidate. "Look at the inscription." She opens it up. *To my Nate, here be the meaning of life! With love, Em.* Jenn shakes her head, still not getting it.

"Look at the date."

"Saint Valentine's Day."

"She gave this to him when they first met. Her broadside at the beach café the other day. They were her opinions, not his. Look underneath."

She has to strain her eyes. It's written in a spidery hand, in pencil. *Sorry. Don't get it. Or you.*

He'd signed it. Yesterday's date. Jenn feels faint.

"Can you give me five minutes, Greg. I'll get ready. We need to start searching for her—properly."

They stare at each other until he nods, his face crumpling

as he turns to the balcony door, its windowpanes rattling in the wind. Beyond, the soar of the sea.

She showers. The water is so cold that she lets out a long, hard stream of piss the moment it hits her skin. She gags at the stench that rises with the steam—must and iron and sex. She soaps herself quickly, recoiling at the stubble springing from her pubic mound. Her arse is hot and swollen to the touch. She rubs her eyes, tries to rub away the pall that fogs her thoughts. It's all there—she can sense it, yet she cannot process it. Emma has gone. Emma, the young radical who has gifted her gormless beau Rousseau for Valentine's—and they'd thought *he* was pulling *her* strings. Would she harm herself over Nathan? It depends what she knows. Would she do it to punish Jenn for the outburst? No. Surely not. Jenn tilts her head back and lets the jet spray her face, her scalp, her mind. No, Emma will be out there, within earshot, witnessing the drama unfold, reveling in the pandemonium that even now she is capable of instigating. Any minute she is going to walk back through those doors and let Greg and Nathan know what a wicked stepmother she has.

As Jenn steps out of the shower she spies a bright red bruise on her breast. A shudder of disgust shivers through her as she pictures him, only hours ago, sucking and biting, wild like a dog. She winces as she tugs her jeans over her damp thighs, and the seam cuts into the puffy folds of her cunt. He'd done her again after the smoke, down by the swimming pool, and then in the kitchen, bent over the table, again and again. She'd let him.

Starving, they'd raided the fridge and devoured the Serrano ham Greg had been keeping for their last day. They peeled it from the waxy paper, strip after strip, and dangled it into each other's mouths. He'd dropped to his knees again and opened her up with his mouth. She clamps a hand to her face as the feel of his tongue, mechanical but efficient, shoots through her. She remembers buckling at the knees; the deck chair being blown across the terrace, the swimming pool lights flickering off, then on, then off for good. She remembers the big front door slamming. Is it possible that Emma came in? Did she see their carnival?

She finds Greg downstairs. He is on the phone, trying to convince the local police to send out a search party for his little girl, but it's futile. She can sense them mocking him.

"*Only* five hours? Isn't that enough? Have you seen the storm out there? I don't care if this is *normal* for Deià—it is not normal for us! My daughter has a fractured ankle and she is out in that hurricane right now."

She wonders whether the officer on the other end of the line will make the connection between the missing girl and the emotional waif they escorted home last night. It is only a matter of time until the events of the past few hours catch up with Jenn. She should come clean before he finds her out. And thinking it through, imagining her confession playing out in front of her, makes her mind up for her. She'll tell him. Now. As soon as he gets off the phone.

He sees her hovering in the doorway, gestures for her to sit down. He gives her an odd look before swiveling his body away from her. He sighs into the phone.

"Yes, I know that, I know we've been through all of that, but what's changed is that I have reason to believe my daughter poses a risk . . . to herself." She feels almost embarrassed for him, she can hear exactly how he must sound to them. Desperate, ridiculous—and every bit the blinkered, indulgent, tourist-father. "No! She is *not* being treated for"—he juts out his jaw, frustrated—" ... *the melancholy*. But there have been some rather big changes in her life these last few weeks." He turns around to eye her again—as though this is just as much for her as the police. "Yes, that's exactly what I'm telling you—and I would like you to alert the coast guard. Yes! *Guarda costas!*" She can hear the officer speaking English. He sounds perfectly bored. After the call has finished, Greg turns to her and says, "So. You heard it."

"What? What did I hear?"

He looks like he might cry. "It's me, Jenn. I've made her ... I should never have confided in her."

She can't go to him. She wants to hold him, but she can't move. "What, Greg? What are you telling me?"

"Well ..." He tries to regain control. He manages a smile and shakes his head. "I've lost my job, for one thing."

Jenn finds herself laughing out of sheer relief. She stems it. "What?"

"I'm sorry. I should have ..." He takes her hand between both of his and squeezes too hard. "The new dean ... Romantics aren't for him, it seems. Aren't for now, full-stop. They've dropped my modules—not just mine, they're making cuts right across the board ..." Jenn just stares at him. There's shock. There's anger. There's an unpleasant stab of hatred. Greg is talking to the floor. "Pouring their funding into New Media."

Jenn releases his hand. "Hang on, Greg, back up—you're telling me they sacked you?"

He shakes his head. He looks more embarrassed than angry. "They demoted me and then they asked me to reapply for my newly demoted post."

"When? When did all this happen?"

He pinches the bridge of his nose. "I didn't want it to spoil the holiday . . . spoil *this*."

He is pointing at the fridge. A shiver of hideous guilt—his precious mountain ham—instantly smothered by anger.

"But . . . you said . . . I thought they were giving you more? More work, more PhD students to supervise?" Her eyes burn into him. He drops his head. "Isn't that what all those calls were about?"

He shakes his head slowly. "No. Those calls were from Chris—telling me I'm a fool. Begging me to reconsider."

She nods, clamps her teeth down on her lower lip. She waits for Greg to look up.

"And you told Emma? You told our fifteen-year-old daughter and not me?"

"It wasn't like that. Emma worked it out for herself. As we're beginning to appreciate, she's not quite the ingenue—"

"She *is*, Greg! She's a fucking child!"

She's weeping, now. Greg crouches in front of her, gently pulls her hands away from her face.

"Darling . . . listen. Emma put two and two together and, I don't know . . . I told her. I'm sorry. I had to tell . . . *someone*. Em made me promise not to tell you. She said you needed a proper holiday more than anyone."

"And this is why you think she's out there now? Because her father lost his job?"

"Yes. I don't know. I think it's part of it, yes. I think there's been a lot of things building up. I think she quarreled with Nathan last night and that was her tipping point—but, yes. Anyway. Now you know." He gets to his feet. He stands there, his eyes low, expecting some sort of rebuke, pathetically grateful when it doesn't come. He kisses her on the forehead. Scoops up the car keys. "I know my daughter, and I have to go and find her." She nods, gets up. He places a hand on her arm, firmly but gently. "Please, can you wait here—I want one of us to be here. For when..." He drops his head again. He opens the door and the wind roars in, knocking a glass over and sending it spinning along the table. It slows to a stop right on the edge. Jenn watches her husband, old, defeated, as he heads out into the dark.

24.

She finds him lying on his bed, reading a magazine. He's plugged into his iPod through one earphone, the other dangling loose against his bare chest. There is something staged about the way he's composed himself, half clad, one leg trailing to the floor, yet he starts when she appears in the doorway. He gives her a panicked look and drops his magazine to the floor, casually knocking it under the bed.

She perches on the edge of the mattress with her back to him. For a while she says nothing. He inches up behind her, loops an arm around her waist, and pulls her down onto his chest. His thumb digs under the side of her bra and finds her nipple. His touch rips through her, as urgent and profound as the first time—but now she fights it. She clamps his hand, pulls it off her. She hauls herself back up and spies the corner of the magazine. He darts a look at her, drops a glance to the floor. On impulse, she sticks the magazine with her big toe and slides it out from under the bed. It's not even porn, it's a lad's mag—some comely wench winking from the cover. Like a schoolteacher examining bad homework, she runs her eye over it, letting him register her contempt. Yet her revulsion is not reserved for the magazine. She's appalled at the recognition and she can't help but feel betrayed by him. She's given him everything she has to give and here he is, carefree, reading the revelations of a soap star's former boyfriend. She's shocked and deflated, and not for the first time today, a worm of doubt eats into her. She thinks, Who are you? What are you to me? And in a flash her betrayal turns to anger.

"How can you just sit here!" She snatches the earphone out. He cowers away from her. She jabs a finger at him. "Why aren't you out there with Greg, looking for her?"

He composes himself, fixes her with those eyes. "Come on, Jenn. You don't believe she's in danger any more than I do. She'll be buzzing now the old man's gone out there trying to rally a search party." Jenn checks the impulse to lash out at him but she lets him know with her eyes: It is not okay; you do not speak about my husband that way. "You said so yourself, Jenn—she's a bad drama queen."

"Possibly. But I'm a bad mother, Nathan." He goes to protest, she holds up a hand. She doesn't want his reassurance; what she wants is the truth. "What happened last night? Tell me."

He flinches away, caught out for a second, but when he turns back he's fully poised again. He's shaking his head, wounded that she could doubt him. He slips his earphones back in—both of them. She gently removes them.

"What happened in the village?"

She gets up, walks to the window. Down below she can see Greg stumbling around the garden with a torch, calling out Emma's name. She steps away.

"I told you."

He's standing level with her now and she can feel her

resolve weakening. Perhaps he is telling the truth. She softens her voice.

"What was the argument about my credit card?"

He looks relieved; steps toward her with a smile.

"Come off it! You know I wouldn't have bought champagne on it, right? I was only winding her up!"

"Winding her up . . ." Jenn can hear the sadness in her own voice. Flat, perfunctory—she can't transmit any anger or any kind of feeling at all. "Winding her up how, Nathan?"

His eyes are darting around her face. He's no longer so sure of himself. He winks at her.

"The champagne! Don't get me wrong, I wouldn't have really ordered it if she'd gone along with it."

"It was *your* idea?"

"Well . . . yeah. No. It's not like it was stealing or anything. Your old man gave us your card."

It squirts through her, hot and squalid. She places her hands on his chest and shoves as hard as she can. He stumbles backward onto the bed and sits there, looking up at her, laughing, but he's scared.

"Emma didn't want to go for the meal, did she?" Menacing, he stands and ducks his face toward her. "She felt bad about taking the card, didn't she, Nathan? Taking from me." She moves her head away, eyes never leaving him. He whips a hand behind her, pulls her close, and kisses her hard on the mouth. He skips past her, pleased with himself.

"You're fucking sexy when you're mad."

He lingers in the doorway with his back to her, one elbow propped up against the jamb for a minute, letting her take her fill of his broad, tanned back, the clumps of muscle around his shoulder blades. "I feel like a shower," he says.

He saunters away, rolling his hips. He is in no doubt—she will take her anger to the shower. She will push him down and ride her fury out. Below, she hears the slam of a car door. The engine starts and the car is crunching, very slowly, along the dirt track. Even in the midst of a crisis, her husband is negotiating each rickety bump and pothole as carefully as he can, in anticipation of the handover back to Eurocar. She listens to him go. She could cry for the love of him.

She refuses eye contact as she passes Nathan and, when he twigs that she's not playing, he follows her down the landing and hooks her from behind with his forearm.

"Get on your knees," he says, grinding his pelvis into her back. His dick is already rigid. He's breathing hard. She just stands there, limp. His hands are all over her tits, pulling, squeezing; his mouth is up and down the nape of her neck, sucking, biting.

She closes her eyes and allows it to douse her one last time, then pushes him away with force. She runs down the stairs.

Nathan screams after her. "You fucking prick tease!" She hears his fist slam into the wall. She catches her breath, waits. His voice comes again, closer. "Where you going?" He's on the bottom stair now. She turns and in that moment is certain.

"I'm going to do the right thing."

He looks young and very afraid as he rubs an earlobe with two fingers and turns down the corners of his mouth ever so slightly. She starts to backpedal out of the room and, before she can change her mind, turns and runs out through the patio doors.

25.

The storm blows great balls of tumbleweeds across the terrace, held up for a moment by the picket fence before their own stalled momentum propels them up and over it, skimming the surface of the swimming pool before coming to rest in the suck of the overflow. Jenn bends into the wind and picks her way across the grove. The ground is littered with small branches and rotting fruit, and with each step she can feel the dogged panic in her chest. She leans against the balustrade, catches her breath. The sea is roaring with a fury she has never heard before, the waves slamming into the beach, throwing great spumes of white up into the blackness. She can still see Greg's taillights as he crawls around the bend, but even at that speed she knows she can't make up the distance—not in this wind, not with her chest.

She forks hard right across the patch of scrub where Benni lights his bonfires—if she's quick, she can intersect Greg on the next bend. She knows what she must do. Once she tells the police what she's done, what she did to her daughter, they'll take it seriously. They'll alert the coast guard. They'll find

Emma and bring her back to her daddy. And then she'll tell him. Everything.

She pushes on, clenches her teeth, and wills herself to go faster. If she can cut him off then there is hope. There is still a way forward. Arms outstretched in the predawn gloaming, she skirts the tangle of myrtle and olive trees that separate the scrub from the road. She narrows her eyes, tries to squint for a space through which to penetrate the switchback. Just ahead is the silhouette of the little wooden ramblers hut, but Jenn cannot see farther than a few feet past it. But then, eureka! The winking indicator as Greg's car pulls out from the lane is now behind her—if she's quick she can wave him down. There's an opening of sorts in the brittle bush, a bar of space where the blackness lifts a little. It's not the makeshift stile onto the road, but there's a gap, just about big enough to squeeze through. She covers her face with her forearms and throws her weight forward, her jumper snagging on the thorns, dragging her back. She yelps, closes her eyes, and goes again, pushing on through the spiky thistle. She shields her face, but the thorns catch her neck, her hair. One tiny talon digs into her neck, holding her fast. She tries to relax, shrinking her head down into her shoulders in an effort to free herself and, as she goes to shift her weight onto her other foot, she slips, skidding down the scree and into the road. She winces as the bramble rips the hair from her scalp, but she can't slow herself. She stumbles right out into the road as Greg speeds past. Hunched over the steering wheel, peering right and left, he seems to look right at her before accelerating into the abyss. She runs after him, waving her arms, hopeless. The brake lights blink bright scarlet before the hairpin bend, then the car slips from view.

26.

The storm has blown itself out as she limps back along the dirt track. As she comes through the broken gate, she stops to watch the shape-shifting hens, bobbing and pecking at the soil in the grove. A sun lounger, illuminated in the pool lights, is half submerged in the water. She drags the two remaining loungers from the lip of the pool and slides them underneath the terrace steps. There's not much point in trying to salvage them now, though. Benni will be up here at first light, assessing the damage, licking his lips at the portion of their damages deposit he can keep.

The darkness is drifting out to silver, and in the mountains, goat bells start up their maudlin chimes. She can't quite countenance this new day and what it will bring. She lingers on the terrace listening to the hum of the fridge inside. Afraid to go in, she paces the grove, retracing her footsteps from last night. Did Emma see them? No. Impossible. Too dark. But she remembers—she tries to shy away from it but she remembers, and she hates it, the noise coming out of her. They'd started quietly, fingers in each other's mouths, but she'd let loose, howling alien, obscene words and thoughts. If Emma had been there, she would have clubbed her with a log.

Jenn is tired; she is changing her mind with each pace this way, each step that. She circles the house and her dead beat mind sets up little trip wires in the half-light. She sees Benni spying on her from behind a shrub. She bustles over—there's nobody there. She steels herself. She'll have to face Nathan sooner or later, and she's suddenly parched. Gingerly she steps inside. There is no sound; nothing here, not a creak from upstairs. The notion that he's drifted off, carefree, listening to his music, enrages her. She swigs orange juice straight from the carton, gulp after gulp. There's only an inch or so left. She catches her breath, ready to finish it off. She spies the slender wrap of Serrano ham stuffed to the back of the fridge like a child might hide a half-eaten cake. She remembers the two of them, lovers, feeding each other. She takes the packet out, despondent, ashamed of herself. There are two slices left. She takes out cling-film and wraps the ham sadly, carefully, then places it back on the shelf next to the olives and Greg's artisanal cheeses. She leans with her back to the fridge and closes her eyes so she can feel its solid weight burring through her. She finishes the orange juice and, aware that she is doing things, mechanically, to put off the moment, she shoves the empty carton in the recycling bag. She is fumbling through her handbag, looking for her phone charger, when the image plays in front of her tired eyes in saturated slow motion. She steadies herself on the cold tiles and stares back at the fridge, the scene of the crime, desperately trying to bring it all back, but yes, she is certain. Vegetarian Nathan was gulping moist mountain ham from her lips.

She takes the stairs, two at time. Her heart is banging. The hippie girl. Monica. All those early-morning jogs. The salt in his hair, on his skin.

In the time it takes her to get to his bedroom two things become clear: Nathan is screwing Monica, and Emma knows. That's where Emma has gone, the hippie cave.

His room is empty; the drawers are open, emptied out. She snatches his wardrobe door open—and though she expects it, even though it's best this way, she is defenseless against the silent howl of rage that splits her in two.

27.

She can see the white heads of the waves slamming into the cliff as she crosses the little wooden bridge. The river-bed, usually bone-dry, is a fierce and racing torrent. From the bridge she can see the rocky cove, fully submerged. It is unthinkable that Emma, with her leg, could have approached the hippie cave from the beach; yet the only other way is via the cliff path—even more dangerous in these conditions. For the first time, Jenn starts to fear for Emma.

A green-pink light is starting to rinse the sky. The stone steps are steep and uneven, hewn from the rock's natural ridges. No way could Emma negotiate these on crutches— and yet some inner motor propels Jenn on. Somehow she knows that this is where Emma's gone. She sits like Emma did, out on the terrace, and shuffles up the steps backward, one at a time, using just one leg to help lever herself up. The last step, a sliver of stone that's not much wider than her foot, is partially blocked by a huge tree trunk, uprooted overnight. If Emma is up there then she went before the storm. Emma didn't see her cavorting, unhinged. Relieved, despising herself, she hauls herself over the trunk and forges onward and upward.

Even in the low light she can see the devastation that the storm has caused. The path is blocked by huge severed branches and the big orbs of rock the uprooted trees have dislodged. She moves slowly, planting each step with caution. The storm has gone, but the terrain still feels vulnerable in its aftermath: Up above, the creak and groan of tree limbs warns her to turn back. But Emma is out there. She knows her girl is there, somewhere.

It's useless. The farther up the cliff path she penetrates, the more dangerous it becomes. She rounds a familiar bend expecting a gentle, staggered skip down to the next level only to find a gaping ocher hole. The path has simply slipped away with the headland. She stands there, beaten. That monumental promontory squats still, devoid of any life, human or animal. She could just stay here and never go back. A gunshot reverberates from the mountains above. Something is moving, then. Life goes on. Jenn holds the slender waist of a sapling with one hand and timidly begins her sideways descent.

She sees the hippie cave and her spirits sink. Even if Emma made it as far as the overhang, it's unthinkable that she could have picked her way down the escarpment, and yet while the light is still low, and for as long as the new day holds off, there's still a flake of hope, she can't give up. She pushes on.

❧

It's daylight by the time she reaches the overhang. A gentle warmth disperses the early-morning mist and there's an apricot sky, promising sunshine soon. Nearby a spring wends down the mountain to the sea, and she's thirsty once more. She kneels and scoops handfuls of cuttingly cold water down her gullet. It seems to sharpen her senses. She should go back. Emma could not have made it this far. And yet the cave is just there, on the other side of the mountain brook. She can smell burned charcoal on the wind, and she knows she must push on. Even if Emma hasn't made it, there are things she needs to hear from Monica.

The way down to the cave is steep but navigable. She sits facing the sea, leans back so that her shoulder blades are almost touching the ground, and slides down the scarp a yard at a time, using the rocks that stud the springy heath as brakes. The sun bursts through the haze as she drops onto the ridge above the cave, and she feels its warmth on her cheeks straightaway. She leans back against an oblong block of rock and shields her eyes from the sun. She can see across the bay into the restaurant where the four of them circled one another that first day. The storm has torn down a chunk of its woven palm-leaf thatch. The matron is sweeping up the debris; trade will be slow today, with the red flag flapping in the wind. She is directly above the cave. She lowers herself down and drops the last couple of feet. At the side of the cave, there's a small wooden ladder nailed into the rock face.

She hesitates, then goes in. The cave is empty. The remnants of a fire still burn, and beside it, an old mattress. Far from the hippie idyll she's conjured, the dank interior is strewn with empty cans and crisp papers. She gags and staggers back out.

She is back on the cliff path, high enough up again to see the police car turn into their drive. It seems symbolic—the silence. The car is moving in fatal slow motion, yet she cannot hear a sound, only the chirrup of chicks, way up above. She steadies herself and breathes slowly, deeply, steeling herself for the worst, when she hears something—just: A sobbing that rises on the wind then fades to silence. She freezes, one of her hands resting on the pine to hold her firm while she strains to make sure. She barely breathes, listening and pleading for the cries to come again; she'd know their cadence anywhere. There is nothing. Her fatigued and foggy conscience has conjured it as succor or a devilish trick. She pushes herself off from the pine and walks on. She is tired. She sorely needs to lie down; yet below the police are knocking at the door and she knows, absolutely, that their call will bring no peace.

It comes again, closer this time. She scans her surroundings, the coarse scrub leading down to the cliff edge; the pine forest above her, leading toward banked terraces of olive trees. She stands still and tries to isolate the source of these cries— then she sees it. There's a casita overlooking a rutted, abandoned olive grove. She's done this walk a hundred times yet never noticed it—no more than a shepherd's hut or a hunter's shelter. It is overhung by gnarled trees and the cracked ground around it is barren, spiked with angry and diminutive thorn trees. The cries come again, more of a hopeless whimper this time, and Jenn is certain she has found her.

28.

The sun dips low on the horizon and, with the cooler air, the beach begins to empty; disparate clumps of people are merging into a single flow as they make their way to the road. Jenn folds up their towels and packs the empty water bottles into the wicker bag. She helps Emma to her feet and casts a glance up at the cave. No one has returned to it since yesterday's storm. They pick their way across the shingle, Emma already adept at negotiating the uneven surface. She hesitates as they pass the beach café. The wizened jewelry vendor throws them an expectant smile but continues packing up. Emma lets Jenn know, with her rueful smile, that she needs to linger for a moment by herself. Jenn gives her shoulder a tender squeeze and walks a little way up the hill. She perches on a rock and waits for her.

From deep in Emma's bag a phone beeps. Jenn stiffens. Its klaxon has been blaring out all day; she could hear it on the beach, and each time her guts would clench. Each time, Emma perfunctorily deleted the message without reading it. Jenn has no idea where he's spent the last twenty-four hours. He could be back in Manchester; it is possible that he's still here in Deià, holed up with his new girlfriend. She suspects that Emma knows and that the answer lies in her bag. She slides her hand in and locates the phone.

❧

Yesterday, in the shepherd's hut, Emma had tried to tell her, but each time she'd broken down in tears. She couldn't face going back to the villa; neither could Jenn, but the late-morning sun seared the tops or their heads through the holes in the roof and forced them back. They made their way slowly through the forest, Emma stalling every so often and succumbing to tears. She barely said a word, but Jenn felt it keenly: her torment, her sadness. There was remorse, too. Neither of them could bring themselves to say it—sorry—but they didn't need to, both of them seemed to know. At the rickety gate, as though winding back time, Emma had set down one of her crutches and extended an arm to Jenn. Jenn ignored the sudden burst of activity on the terrace above; she slid her fingers through Emma's and squeezed. Sorry. I love you.

Emma slept for the rest of the day, although Jenn suspected that this was as much to avoid her father's probing as fatigue catching up with her. She appeared on the terrace shortly after he'd left for the village. She sat down at the table, poured herself a glass of wine, and indicated with a nod that she was ready to talk.

❧

It wasn't the first time. It had happened once before, not long after they started dating. She pulled pints in his local.

She wasn't even pretty, and somehow that hurt more than the betrayal itself. He denied it, even now he could never admit to it, but she knew, everyone knew. And a part of her blamed herself: It served her right for being so uptight, so damn cautious. The week before they came away, Nathan gave her an ultimatum: If she didn't love him enough to make that sort of commitment, then he didn't see any point in his coming to Deià with her. They did it the night before they came away. She could forgive him for the bartender but she could never, ever forgive him for Monica.

❧

Jenn lets the phone fall from her grip and slide back into the bag. She is stricken with remorse, then self-loathing. It hits her in waves.

Tomorrow they will go home, the three of them. There is nothing she wants more.

The last of the beach traffic has left by the time Emma limps into view. She is surprised and pleased that Jenn has waited. As she gets closer it's clear she's been crying, but she looks better for it.

They can hear the spit and crackle of a bonfire as they reach the path, still strewn with tree bark. Greg is chatting with Benni. He is standing with his back straight, purposeful. He's holding a sheaf of papers in one hand and with the other he is tossing them, one at a time, into the flames. There is no hint of the ill mood that Benni's presence usually begets. Greg's nodding his head in slow, considered acceptance of whatever Benni is telling him. Jenn suspects her husband is making his peace. They will not be returning to Villa Ana next year.

Greg raises a hand in greeting as he hears the scrape of the gate on the gravel; Benni turns around, steps a little way from Greg. He gives Jenn a sheepish look then scuttles off with his rake to the other side of the lemon grove. Greg turns to smile at them as they come alongside him.

"Nice day?" he asks.

"Gorgeous," Jenn says. Her eyes are still trained on Benni. He looks back over his shoulder as though sensing her watching him. "Although the sun would have been insufferable without that breeze from the sea."

"Mmm," Emma says, and leans her head on Jenn's shoulder. "It was good just to be able to kick back and do nothing." She gestures to her plastered leg. "You do realize I'm going to have a two-tone leg for the rest of the year."

The three of them laugh. Benni is walking down the path to his van, smiling. He throws them a wave and the little stub of anxiety in Jenn's chest fades to nothing.

"How about you, señor?" Jenn nods at the incinerated papers, burned to flaking charcoal. "That's not what I think it is, is it?"

"It is *precisely* what you think it is," he declares. He sees Emma's face fall and snorts. "Couldn't figure out how to end it. It's pretty execrable actually."

"Shouldn't you let someone else be the judge of that?" Jenn asks him.

"Not this time," Greg says, and shuffles across to Emma so all three of them are in a row, watching it burn to ash.

Jenn is conscious of the moment: the slow dissipation of the day; the sun, a dried-blood red; the three of them, healing.

"Right, I'm off to bathe before dinner," Emma says. She

gives Jenn a hopeful look. "Can you help me get in and out?"
Jenn nods, smiles. "Where we going, again?"

Greg gives them a teasing, inscrutable smile. Emma pokes him.

"Come on, Dad! Where have you booked? A girl needs to know what to wear, for goodness' sake!"

He shakes his head. "This is one place we don't need to book." Jenn tries to catch his eye. There's something about him—he's reborn, and she likes it. His eyes dance on Emma as he playfully smacks her on the backside.

"Wear what you like. But be quick about it!"

Emma leans on Jenn's shoulder and they start up the path to the villa, but Greg catches up with them. He touches Jenn's elbow, signals for her to hang back. She gives Emma a smile.

"You go on up, darling. I'll give you a hand in a minute."

Greg waits until Emma is out of earshot.

"I've spoken with Chris."

"Yes?"

"I've made a decision. I'm not going back."

Jenn nods, unsure what to say. She smiles, tries to project confidence. "Good . . . good. I'm glad." She wraps her arms around his big solid frame. "It's going to be fine, Greg. I promise."

She closes her eyes tight and lays her face flat along his broad chest.

※

Jenn takes the white cotton dress from the hanger; it still has the label intact. She snips it off with the nail scissors, slips the dress on. She sits at the dressing table and fixes her hair. Tonight she'll wear it up, just how Greg likes it. As she pins it in place she sees that around her temples a few stray grays are starting to poke through. She drags one out above her head and picks up the nail scissors but then stops herself. She fancies that this time she might live with them for a while, see how she gets on.

Jenn and Emma sit on the terrace drinking wine, smoking. They can hear Greg getting ready upstairs. Footfall sails closer to the balcony above, and Emma quickly passes the cigarette to Jenn. They hear him move back into the bathroom and Jenn passes it back, winking.

The darkness is deepening, the air is cooling. They can hear Greg trimming his beard. They smile at each other and take a ginger swig of their wine—Jenn a split second after Emma. Stars are pinning the sky. The metronomic burr of cicadas breezes out in ripples, cuts to silence, then starts up again. Last night, flushed with brandy, Greg had told them how the male cricket makes that noise by running the top of one wing against the bottom of the other. "Like they're crying?" Emma said. "No, not at all," he'd replied. "Like they're washing their hands of someone."

The moon climbs above the mountains, low and swollen. Finally they hear Greg locking the shutters. Jenn corks the wine bottle and scatters the cigarette ash in the grass, wiping down the saucer with her thumb.

Greg strides out onto the terrace. He's wearing his linen jacket with jeans and loafers—no socks. Jenn catches his eye, puckers an air kiss at him. She helps Emma into the car.

They reach the top of the switchback and fork right for Deià. She leans her head coquettishly on his bicep.

"Greg, how thoughtful . . . you're taking us to El Olivio!"

He stares straight ahead—steely. "Not this time."

They drive on through the village. They spot Benni on the pavement outside Bar Luna. Greg taps the horn with the base of his palm and Benni sees the car and ducks down to meet the window as they pass. Jenn throws him a little wave but he looks right through her and trains his eyes on Greg. Benni removes his pipe from his mouth and presses his lips together in a gesture of what? Jenn cannot be sure, but her shoulders give out a little quiver of unease. She thinks back to the two of them, by the bonfire, their heads bent as one. Is it possible that he saw? She flips her head over her shoulder expecting to see Benni standing in the road, watching their car tail away, but he's already mounting the steps of Bar Luna. She relaxes a little. Whatever they were talking about, whatever she imagines they talked about, it wasn't her. They passed Jaume, and she's relieved, if a little sad that they're not paying one last visit to Miki's wonderful place. They head out past Sa Pedrissa and it suddenly dawns on her—the roadside restaurant they're always promising to visit. Of course! The little car labors up the hill then, as they coast its crest and begin their descent toward the garage, Greg slips into fifth gear and motors past the café.

She can't help herself. A panic pricks at her armpits. She can just make out the faint odor of fear sweat. There's only really Valldemossa they could be heading for—scene of his first betrayal. She can hack it, she thinks; she can put a brave face on it. If Emma can, then she can.

Gregory slows past the garage and waits at the junction

as though prolonging her agony. He turns right and now she knows where he's heading. There can be only one place. Her throat starts to tighten.

The darkness closes in, impenetrable. The road dips and coils. He clicks his full beams on. Emma's head appears in the space between the front seats.

"Come on, Dad! Where are we? Where are you taking us?"

Greg darts his eyes at Jenn, before focusing on Emma in the rearview mirror.

"I doubt you'll remember it, darling. But you loved it!"

Jenn's heart is banging.

"Where?" squeals Emma.

He turns to Jenn. "Your mother knows. She had a sandwich there the other evening, didn't you, Jenn?" Her fingers open and close, open and close, against her thigh. His eyes move back to the road. "Go on, tell her."

"I think we're going to Paco's, Em."

Greg smiles and shifts into a lower gear as they make their descent into Banyalbufar.

Acknowledgments

I wrote this book during a period of instability and penury. I would not have been able to write it without the patience and encouragement of my husband, who threatened divorce if I didn't ditch the day job and finish the novel.

I am hugely indebted to Deborah Schneider and Jonny Geller for lighting that first spark; to Alison Callahan, my rather brilliant and merciless editor, for sharpening my quill and spicing up my ink; and to Bill Thomas, Melissa Danaczko, and James Melia for their ongoing support and enthusiasm.

I would like to thank my father, who first taught me the value of time; and my mother, for her generosity of spirit.

I would also like to thank Oscar of B.C. for friendship and for pestering me to ditch the pipe in favor of a finger of fudge. "To art is freedom."

About the Author

Helen Walsh was born in Warrington, England, in 1976. Her second novel, *Once Upon a Time in England,* was the winner of a Somerset Maugham Award. She now lives in Liverpool.

A Note About the Type

The text of this book is set in Metropolitan Roman, a font designed by Colin Kahn for the Lanston Type Company in 2005. It is based on the work of Bruce Rogers and Frederic Warde.